A New Life
By: Alexander Martin

Chapter One: Finding Out

I came home early to pick up a few things for an afternoon meeting at one of the houses I was showing when I noticed Benjamin's car in the driveway.

My husband Benjamin was a high-profile prosecution lawyer in our city, hell, most of the state. He had never lost a case, and seeing his car at home so early in the afternoon was not something I expected.

'Maybe he's working from home today,' I thought as I walked inside.

It didn't take long for me to figure out what was happening. The smell in the air wasn't my perfume, and sounds were coming from the upstairs bedroom.

'Thirty-Seven years,' I thought to myself as I gained the strength to climb the stairs. I had never cheated on Benjamin, not once, not even flirted with another man.

We had been together since the last year of high school. I had been with him through everything.

Thirty-seven years we had been married, but we had known each other for two years before that, and now it was all getting thrown away.

I wanted to see who he deemed worthy of throwing such a life away.

My eyes were in shock as I peeked into our bedroom. Fifty-five-year-old Benjamin was screwing Charlize, my best friend's youngest daughter. Her petite body bounced up and down on him as she rode him hard.

I stood there in total shock, not able to move. Benjamins was fifty-five, about to turn fifty-six. Charlize had just celebrated her twentieth birthday just a few days ago. The petite blonde rode him like he was the last Bronco at the stables.

I wanted to burst in there and catch them in the act, but I remembered what Benjamin always preached; it was what they could prove, not what they saw.

I took out my phone and started recording every word, every sentence. I angled the phone just inside the doorway so they couldn't see me.

'Shit,' I thought as they finally stopped.

He had just cum inside her and bragged about how he loved how she felt on top of him. Luckily for her, Benjamin could no longer produce children, or she might be pregnant. Through their talks, I realized this wasn't the first time they had fucked in our bed.

'Keep talking,' I thought as I heard him talking about me and how I had become a prude in my old age.

I was turning fifty-four, and as far as I was concerned, he was the one that was becoming less sexual; I wanted more, and he seemed to want less, and now I knew why. He was getting it from an outside source.

I moved into the guest room as they took a break and wandered downstairs. I took the opportunity to silence my phone and text, Alexander, letting him know something had come up and I wouldn't make the meeting. He knew me well enough to know it had to be important if I missed a meeting. He quickly responded, letting me know it was okay.

I looked at our smart home app and saw them in the kitchen through our home cameras; I always wondered why he would delete the camera's storage daily, he always said it was to save room for if anything happened, but now I knew it was because he was cheating.

They came back up the stairs and quickly resumed. Benjamin would've seen my car if he had only looked out the living room window.

They continued in various positions for almost an hour before I knew I had enough evidence to damn him and his upcoming political career.

I slowly made my way back downstairs and stood in the kitchen. I saved all the camera activity to the cloud and what I recorded on my phone.

Another half-hour passed, and I heard them finishing up. Slowly they came downstairs and didn't notice me standing in the kitchen behind them. As Charlize turned around to kiss my husband goodbye, she gasped loudly.

"Wrap up. It's cold out there," I said as I sipped my soda.

"Ms. Hooper," Charlize said in shock.

"After two hours, you don't have to call me that," I nodded.

Benjamin stared at me and then at the phone on the kitchen counter.

"As well as the others," I nodded, looking at the cameras all over the house. "Safely stored on my cloud."

"I will take care of this," Benjamin tried to assure Charlize.

"Sent a copy to your mom as well," I smiled as Charlize opened the door.

"Ben!" Charlize cried as he walked her out.

I heard her sobbing as he tried to console her, but I knew it was a show. Benjamin knew he was screwed. Slowly he walked back inside and poured himself a drink at the bar.

"Two hours?" he asked as he approached me.

"Yup," I nodded.

"Not a single word?" Benjamin asked, staring at the phone.

"Proof, not words, remember," I smiled.

Benjamin nodded. "Who else did you send it to?" he asked.

"All the kids, Alexander, Trevor, and Bernice," I nodded.

"Fuck!" Benjamin yelled as he launched my phone across the kitchen.

I watched as it bounced, and the screen cracked as it landed a few feet from me.

"Can say that again, the kids were on a voice call just now," I said, staring down at it.

"Still am," Mason said.

The rest chimed in afterward.

Mason and Dawson were our oldest twin brothers. Then there was Debra, the middle, and Sheila, the youngest.

"Fuck, fuck, fuck!" Benjamin shouted as he stomped on the phone until it was in tiny pieces.

The house phone rang. "Going to destroy that too?" I asked.

"See you in court!" Benjamin yelled as he stormed out of the house.

There was the fork in our marriage. I don't know what I was expecting, but I thought he would feel remorse for his actions.

"I am fine," I answered, knowing it was Sheila.

She was my baby girl, constantly checking on her mom, and unlike the others who were in different states, Sheila didn't leave far from home when she left.

Mason took off for the military as soon as he could sign up, which led to his dad being proud of him, but then he left before getting kicked out due to his temper. Just like Benjamin, he was prone to violence once he got mad. Now he lived with his best friend in Kansas.

Dawson was always the levelheaded one of the family and took after his father and went into law. He was a defense lawyer and lost many times. But he loved every minute of it, and I knew he was happy with his new wife, Pamela. They lived in South Carolina.

Debra was the mother hen of the group. She always knew everything about every one of them. She always checked on them and ensured everyone, especially Mason, stayed out of trouble. She married early, at nineteen, to her high school sweetheart Jimmy. They had three kids and lived in Florida.

Then there was the baby of the bunch, the rebel of the group. Sheila was attending a community college and not majoring in anything important, which drove Benjamin crazy.

Mason was in construction, Dawson had the law practice, Debra was a stay-at-home mom and homeschooled her kids, while Sheila had no plans for her future. She lived forty minutes away in a small apartment.

"I talked to the others, they are on their way," Sheila said. "I am finishing here then I will come and spend the night."

I was in no mood to turn down the company. I had spent weeks, even months, alone at home with the kids in this house, but now as the shadows crept in as the sun went down, it seemed lonely and dark.

"Thank you," I said as I hung up.

Bernice texted me and told me she would make dinner and bring it around if I wanted to eat. I felt terrible, it was her daughter in the video I sent her, but I was sure she felt just as immoral because her daughter ruined my marriage.

I was surprisingly not mad at Charlize. After all, she wasn't the home wrecker. She was just along for the ride. I was angry at Benjamin. He could have told me he wasn't happy in the marriage, and I would have given him the divorce. Now I was going to fight him tooth and nail.

Sheila eventually came around, and I was glad to see her blonde hair walk through the door. Sheila was smiling at me. I had talked to the others while she was on the way over.

"You're going to be single," Sheila said as she put her coat away.

"Don't," I said as I sat on the couch.

"A hot Gilf, hot on the prowl," Sheila said as she jumped on the couch beside me. "Or are you going to be a cougar?"

"A what and what the hell is a Gilf?" I asked.

"Grandma I would like to fuck," Sheila said, shaking her head at me. "And a cougar is a female that goes after younger males, for partners."

"No and definitely not," I said, shaking my head. "Let's get through the divorce before you start planning to take me out and show me around," I said as I looked at her.

I had no plans of jumping back into the dating pool. If things went as I thought they would, I wouldn't need to work, but I knew I wouldn't want to be like one of those women who stayed home and did nothing.

The conversation continued, but eventually, I got tired and headed to the upstairs guestroom to go to bed. I couldn't lie in my bed knowing what I knew. Benjamin and his twenty-year-old mistress's images were still stuck in my head.

I WOKE UP TO THE SOUNDS of all my children in the house. I knew I shouldn't think of them as children anymore. They were all full-grown adults with their own lives and own problems.

I got up and headed downstairs to meet them.

Even though Mason and Dawson were twin brothers, you couldn't tell by looking at them, it would take a few glances to see the resemblance, but most people thought they were brothers, but never twins.

Mason was slightly taller than Dawson, and he was a gym rat, always in the gym, ate perfectly, and it showed. He was muscular all over and had the body of a bodybuilder.

While Dawson was the opposite, he loved his carbs and sweets. So he was round, in all the wrong places. He wasn't overly obese, but he was trending in that direction if he didn't start to reign on his bad habits.

They both had brown mousey hair. Mason cut his short, while Dawson liked growing his out.

Then there was Debra, who was the spitting image of me. Dark brown hair, plump in every way. We weren't fat or chubby, just as the saying went, very thick in all the right places. She was the same height as me at five-eight.

Sheila was the odd duck; there were times after she was born when Benjamin had thought I had cheated on him. What a crock of shit.

Sheila had blonde hair and was more of an athlete than a gym rat. She liked to run, play football, basketball, and hockey.

Sheila wanted to play every sport, and she was good at it. None of the boys could keep up with her once she got started. She was also naturally tanned, another thing none of us had. We were all pale as ghosts.

It wasn't until we looked further into Benjamin's family that we saw the resemblance to a great-grandmother who was Sicilian. That's when he stopped saying that Sheila wasn't his daughter.

Benjamin was hardly ever active in their lives, except for Mason. The day Mason left for the military, Benjamin was ecstatic now; the two barely talked, and I guessed that would only worsen.

"You okay?" Debra asked as I entered the living room.

"Yes, I am fine I got cheated on, I didn't get into a wreck," I said, sitting on the couch.

"We know, it's just so sudden," Dawson said.

"Sudden, my ass, Ben has been acting up the moment we all left," Mason said from standing by the window.

"He's not coming back," I shook my head. "And if he did you're not allowed to hit him," I said, looking at Mason. "Any of you," I said, looking over at Sheila.

"I wasn't going to hit him, just knee him in the nuts," Sheila smiled.

"Both of those are the same thing," Dawson said. "I already started getting a case together."

"You will lose," I said as I looked at Dawson. "You're on a winning streak, don't jeopardize it on this, I can handle your father."

"You sure?" Dawson asked.

"Absolutely; I have been dealing with him for a long time. I know how to beat him," I nodded. "Speaking of which," I said as the home phone rang.

I knew it had to be him, only family members had the home phone number, and everyone else was here.

"We need to talk," Benjamin said.

"Asshole!" Sheila shouted.

"They are all there?" Benjamin asked.

"Yup, I wouldn't show your face up here, unless you want Mason's fists hitting it," I said.

"Agreed," Benjamin said. Although I told him not to, he knew his son, Mason, would hit his father.

"The usual place?" I asked.

"In an hour?" Benjamin asked.

"I just got up, make it two," I nodded.

"Okay, see you then," I said as I hung up.

"We are coming with you," Debra said as they stood beside me.

"Seriously, I am fine," I nodded. "I was taken back and now the reality of my situation has hit me and I am fine, these things happen."

IT TOOK A BIT MORE to put it through to them, but they all said they would be here when I got back, and they were a phone call away.

I got ready to go, making sure I wasn't wearing anything that would give Benjamin a hint that I wanted to stay any longer than needed.

I walked out of my car and saw Sheila sitting inside. I sighed as I got in, "I should have known," I said as I started it up.

"Spare key, remember?" Sheila said, dangling the spare key in her fingers.

"You snuck out," I nodded.

"Please, I have been sneaking out of that house since I was fourteen," Sheila smiled.

I knew better than to argue with her. She was my baby girl, after all. Even as a child, she clung to my legs when I walked around the house. With the others, the first day of school was a chore to get them to go to school. For Sheila, it was an absolute nightmare. She screamed and hollered. It sounded like I was torturing the poor child.

I did nothing different with her, some kids are more physically bonded to a parent than others, and that was my Sheila. I didn't mind these days as she was more of a best friend than most other friends.

I pulled up to our spot, a hole-in-the-wall breakfast place. It looked like a dump from the outside, but it served the best bagel sandwiches in the city.

"You're not coming inside," I said as I put my foot down.

"I have a good view of him from here," Sheila said, patting her hip.

"You are not going to shoot your father," I said, shaking my head.

"Depends on him," Sheila smiled.

I shook my head and walked inside. Benjamin was sitting in our usual spot, and the place was empty, which was never a thing.

"How much?" I asked as I sat down across from him.

"More than they make in a day," Benjamin said as he looked at me.

"Gabriel," I smiled as the owner came over. "Double it, he can afford it, and it's a Friday, you should have asked for a lot more," I said.

Benjamin's eyes went wide.

"I can leave, Sheila's in the car and well she patted her hip, so you know what that means," I said as I looked over at Benjamin.

"Fine, double it," Benjamin sighed.

"Now we can talk," I nodded.

Gabriel had been in business here longer than most of the others. We first came here the morning after our honeymoon was over and have been coming ever since.

"Out of all of them, the liberal is the one that carries her gun everywhere," Benjamin shook his head.

"Mason doesn't need to carry, no one will start a fight with him," I smiled. "Dawson, well Dawson lives in a fantasy world where calories don't add to your weight, Debra leaves hers in the car, her husband is the one that brings it everywhere, and Sheila takes after her mum, she just owns a lot more than I do," I smiled.

Gabriel brought out our usual and returned behind the scenes leaving us alone.

"What will it take?" Benjamin asked.

"For all of it to disappear so that we can have a quiet divorce and I keep my mouth shut?" I asked.

"And the kids," Benjamin stated.

"Ha, good luck with that," I shook my head. "Debra is a stay-at-home mom with more social media friends than most teenagers. I am sure that video is trending as we speak."

"Fuck me, why did you have to send it to them?" Benjamin asked.

"Never leave your proof in one hand, spread it around to make sure it's...." I started to say.

Benjamin slammed his hand on the table. "Will you stop quoting me?"

"Chest," I said as I smiled at him.

"What?" Benjamin asked before looking down at the red dot on his chest.

"She's a really good shot, but you did teach her, so you know that," I said calmly, eating.

Benjamin slowly nodded, and the dot went away. "She would, wouldn't she?" Benjamin asked.

"You remember that first day of school?" I asked.

Benjamin nodded.

"To answer your question, it's simple. Take back the feeling I had walking in and seeing my husband having sex with someone half my age. Take that image out of my head, so I don't see it anymore, and then find me a place in the house where I don't hear the names you called me while fucking your mistress. Do all that, and we can talk."

Benjamin looked down at his plate. "I can't do any of that, and ...."

"Don't," I said, shaking my head. "You're not sorry, you're upset and angry that you got caught and now it could jeopardize your political career. Did Stanley tell you to get ahead of this before it gets out?"

I mentioned the mayor's name as he was the one that publicly stood behind Benjamin as he announced his run for politics.

"If this gets out it will ruin me," Benjamin said.

"No, it will help you," I said, standing up. "You will be like all the other politicians, corrupt, immoral and inept of keeping promises. You want this to go away, you shouldn't have stuck your cock up a twenty-year old's ass."

Benjamin shook his head.

"I got that part on the video also. She is quite vocal with a cock up her ass," I said as I put a flash drive on the table. "Sharing evidence with you. That has everything on it, in case you want to see what you look like from a different angle."

"I didn't intend to hurt you, that is the truth," Benjamin said as he quickly held my hand.

"Charlize is twenty years old," I said, looking down at him. "You held her in your arms the day they brought her home. When Martin left Bernice, you promised her you would help care for them. Did you have those thoughts when you were changing her as a baby?"

"Come on, that's sick!" Benjamin said.

"Well, that's what I see when I look at her," I said.

"Alison, you're blowing this way out of proportion," Benjamin said, shaking his head.

"Oh, blowing, that's on the video as well," I smiled. "Seems that she does a much better job of blowing your cock, than when she blew on that breathalyzer test a few weeks after she got her driving license."

"Okay," Benjamin said as he stood up. "I can see you can't have a civil conversation."

Benjamin stormed past me as he headed for the door.

"Her favorite color was dark green because it matched the color of your car, she was ten at that time!" I yelled at him as he opened the door.

Sheila walked inside as I sat back down. "You, okay?" she asked as she sat across from me.

I shook my head. I was putting on a strong face, but inside I was crumbling. "How can I face him in court?"

"You've stood up to him many times," Sheila said.

I wiped my eyes. "Thanks for coming," I nodded.

"We will all be there, with you," Sheila nodded. "Dawson could...."

"Benjamin would have a field day with Dawson," I shook my head. "It has to be me. No one else will step foot in a courtroom against your father, and he knows it."

"You do know all of his quotes," Sheila laughed.

I laughed along with her. "They really do work," I smiled as we got up. "Make sure he pays you for the full day!" I said to Gabriel as we left.

Chapter Two: Facing the Truth

I walked into my office with a headache. Worrying about what Benjamin would say or do kept me up most of the night.

Sheila stayed with me for the second time while the others booked hotel rooms. No doubt they wanted their privacy.

Alexander greeted me at the door with a hug, "Thanks," I said as I went to my desk.

"He tried to bribe me," Alexander said as he stood near my desk.

"Of course, he did," I shook my head. "What did he offer, and what did he want?"

"He wanted me to keep my mouth shut about the video you sent, as well as to trash talk you," Alexander said.

Benjamin knew that Alexander and I had been working for nearly ten years. He bought the houses, his son Derek renovated them, and I got them decorated and ready to be sold. It was a good arrangement. An arrangement that benefited everyone.

I shook my head. Alexander would never trash-talk me to anyone, let alone for the sake of my soon-to-be ex-husband, that cheated on me.

I knew Benjamin was reaching at straws now. He was becoming desperate. I had all the leverage, and he wanted something on me to keep me from finishing what he had started after the moment he closed the most prominent case in his career.

Benjamin wanted, no, he needed to be the best. Since the day I met him, he has strived to win my heart. There were plenty of others. But Benjamin wanted to beat them all to get the bustiest young woman in the school.

It worked. Benjamin won me over in a couple of weeks, and after a few years, we were married.

Now, he wanted to run for political office, preferably a seat in Congress. I was the only thing stopping him, and I knew how he was; Benjamin saw me as a threat, and threats had to be eliminated.

'Damn,' I thought as I knew Benjamin would try to threaten poor Charlize. I knew she was the one that was part of this all, but she didn't deserve to be endangered.

I called Bernice and asked for Charlize's phone number.

"Meet me," I said as she answered.

"Where?" Charlize asked.

I selected a spot where it would be very public and less likely to draw attention. I requested the rest of the day off to ensure everything was in order before the court date.

"FIRST," CHARLIZE SAID as she met me at the café. I stopped her dead in her tracks.

"This meeting is about the upcoming court date, nothing more," I said as I looked at her doe eyes staring back at me. "I don't care about how you feel and how sorry you are," I said, setting the ground rules.

Charlize took a seat and nodded.

"Good," I said as I looked over at her. "When did it start?" I asked.

"Just over a year ago," Charlize answered promptly.

That hit like a dagger straight to the heart. I had sex with Benjamin during that time. If I knew he was fucking around on me, I would have. I stopped myself there. I couldn't have known, and thinking about the past wasn't something I wanted to do.

"How often?" I asked.

"Anytime he was away, or if you were gone for a long time," Charlize answered.

"Weekly, then," I nodded.

"Yes," Charlize replied.

"Gifts, clothes, any of the sort?" I asked.

"Plenty, also weekly," Charlize nodded as she looked down at the notepad, I was writing in.

"Just at the house or other places?"

"Mostly your house, but a couple of times, hotels, and resorts, he took me on vacation last winter," Charlize answered.

"He told me he was going to a convention," I said as I remembered that event.

"Yes, it was boring, I was there with him, but it was only for one day, then we went.... Well, we went somewhere else," Charlize said.

"I see," I nodded.

I came here wanting answers, and Charlize gave me more than I needed.

"My mom told me to tell you everything," Charlize said. "I haven't answered any of his calls, or ...."

I held my hand up. "I don't need to know," I said. "What happens now is between you and him, I just need this information before he threatens you not to talk to me."

"I wouldn't do that," Charlize said. "He told me that the two of you were separating this year."

"Well, he wasn't wrong," I chuckled.

"May I ask something?" Charlize asked.

"Sure," I nodded.

"How is Sheila taking it?" Charlize asked.

I shook my head and stared back at her. "If I, were you, I would avoid Sheila as much as possible."

"I see," Charlize nodded.

The rest of the meeting went well. Charlize answered all my questions without hesitation and got me all the information I needed to know and then some.

I bid her farewell and told her to stay away from Benjamin as I knew he would try to manipulate her.

I went to the gym afterward to clear my head. I always thought better after a bit of a workout. As I left, I saw Benjamin standing by my car.

"What?" I asked.

"Papers," Benjamin said, handing me the divorce papers.

"Oh no," I said as I declined to receive them. "You're not getting off that easily."

I knew that he wanted a quick divorce out of the courtroom, but he was the one that said he would see me in court, so that's what we were going to do.

"Alison!" Benjamin shouted as I put my things in the truck. "Why?"

"Why fuck her, every week?" I shouted back. "You bought her gifts and took her on vacation, sometimes, right under my nose, and in our house, in our bed!"

Benjamin shook his head. "Cheating happens, I was bored, and unhappy she was there," he said. "We haven't been that intimate in months!"

"You have been screwing her for over a year!" I said, staring at him. "A year!"

Benjamin shook his head as he stared at me. "You're going to ruin me," he said as he pleaded for me to take the papers.

I pushed them back at him. "You should've thought about that before sticking your dick where it doesn't belong!" I said as I opened the door. "If you weren't happy, you could have told me, we could have gone our separate ways peacefully, I wouldn't have fought you."

"That's what scared me," Benjamin said. "You would've left, and I would...."

"Be just fine," I shook my head. "You can't have it your way all the time, sometimes you do lose."

I left Benjamin in the parking lot, he was running out of options, and he knew it.

Luckily, he had a few more weeks before the court date, which he scheduled, not me.

EVERYBODY RETURNED home after a week of checking and rechecking that I was alright. Sheila was the only one that didn't have to board a plane. The others told her to keep an eye out for me.

Showing homes always made me relax, and this one was no different. It was a large ranch-style house with a vast backyard in an up-and-coming neighborhood way out of the city limits.

As people came into the house on the date I set for the open house. I started thinking about getting a place like this for myself. A new start, new neighborhood, new furniture. In essence, a new me.

The more I thought about it, the more I wanted a new start. Except for the job, I loved my job, but I could do it with a fresh start on many other things. Especially a house, that sizeable two-story house, would be too big for me now.

'Great,' I thought as I saw one of Benjamin's friends walk in.

"Stuart," I said, meeting him in the kitchen.

"Alison," he nodded.

"Didn't know you were in the market for a new house," I said as others walked around.

"It crossed my mind, a time or two," Stuart smiled.

'Bullshit!' I thought. Stuart owned three houses and a few rentals; he had no reason to buy another.

"Cut to the chase. I have clients," I said as the room cleared.

"The house, the rental, and the fishing lodge, all yours and a substantial amount, just to walk away and sign the papers," Stuart said as he pulled out a large vanilla envelope.

I laughed. "It's going to cost him a lot more than that," I said.

"Alison, come on," Stuart said.

"He was fucking a twenty-year old in my bed for over a year!"

"And he is sorry," Stuart pleaded. "Don't ruin the man because he had an affair," he shrugged. "Everyone is having or thinking about having an affair, just because they don't...."

"There, right there, carry on, don't stop," I smiled. "They don't go through with it. Of course, I have had thoughts about it, but I have never acted on it."

"So, you're saying you are better than him?" Stuart asked.

"Better, no," I smiled as someone passed. "Loyal, most definitely, I didn't spread my legs at the first time that I wanted to screw someone, that I found attractive."

"Alison," Stuart said, shaking his head.

"Did you, or have you?" I asked, looking at Stuart. "Have you cheated on Mandy?"

"Our marriage isn't in question," Stuart said, shaking his head.

"My god, you have," I said, shaking my head. "Was it with a twenty-year old? One of Charlize's friends?"

"No! stop it!" Stuart barked.

I knew that look; I had caught him. "You better leave," I nodded. "If you can't look me straight in the face, there is no chance you can mediate between the two of us."

"Fine," Stuart retreated.

"Tell Nadine I said hi," I said as he left.

"I will..., "he stopped and looked at me.

I knew it had to be Charlize's friend Nadine that Stuart was seeing behind his wife's back. She was more outgoing than most of the other friends.

"Fuck!" Stuart shouted as he stormed out.

'What's with these men?' I thought.

Mandy didn't deserve to be cheated on; she was the picture-perfect housewife. Of course, she was a tad older than me, and Stuart was older than Benjamin, but that did mean he had to cheat on her.

THE OPEN HOUSE WAS a huge success. After a few days of the house being on the market, I sold it for a considerable profit, which made Alexander happy and myself.

Working extra hours made me take my mind off everything that was happening, and for a change, I didn't feel like I should rush home to be with someone or make someone dinner. It was pretty satisfying that I knew it would all be over soon.

What hadn't stopped was Benjamin's attempts to bid for me, allowing him to walk away. I even got a notice from the mayor's office to sit down and talk with him. I denied it.

They could all go down together. I knew if Benjamin was willing to go to these lengths, he had nothing on me.

What could he have? Was I lousy in bed? Was I a terrible cook? All of these were lies. We had four kids, and if we didn't get things taken care of so that we wouldn't have any more kids, I knew there would be many more of them.

As for the cooking, there was more of him these days than when we first married.

"He's at it again," Kelly said as she returned from lunch.

I shook my head as I saw Derek entering the office.

Unlike his father, who was a man of his word and a pillar of the community. Derek was a horndog, the rumor was that he wanted to fuck every woman he met, but I didn't believe it until I went to one of the houses he was working on and saw him fucking one of the helpers.

That image and the other images of my husband were now locked inside my head for good.

"One day you will say yes," Derek smiled as he looked at Kelly.

"One day I will sue you," Kelly replied.

"He will stop," I said as I looked at Derek, who jumped at the sound of my voice. "Won't you!"

"I thought you were still out," Derek said as he looked around our small office for his father.

"I've been back for a while now," I said as I stared a hole through him. "Your father is out, what do you want?"

"One of the contractors is asking for more, and the Cherokee house needs permits," Derek said, leaning against my desk.

"Permits," I said, handing him the papers. "Which contractor?" I asked.

"Deadland," Derek answered. "So, when's the big day?"

"Three weeks," I answered as I looked up the contractor.

"Nervous?" Derek asked.

"Leave her alone," Kelly said from across the room.

"It's okay," I nodded. "No, I am not. He is in the wrong. I am in the right. There is no reason to be nervous."

"Depends," Derek said as he lifted one of the unicorn paperweights I had on my desk and tossed it up and down in his hand. I loved unicorns and collected figurines. "If it's a male judge and he takes one look at Charlize, he might understand why the old man did it," Derek said as he looked over at Kelly.

"She's young, that's all," Kelly said.

"He means that Charlize has a cheerleader's body, tight muscle toned and long legs, with blonde hair," I said.

"And a tight little ass, that begs to be...." Derek made the motions of fucking.

I shook my head. "Well too bad she turned you down and fucked Benjamin," I smiled.

"Guess the old man has better moves than you do," Kelly laughed.

"He has more money and more popularity, that's all," Derek said as he stood up and put the unicorn down.

"Not what I heard," Kelly smiled.

I laughed as I knew she was playing on his ego. "He did go for over two hours," I smiled.

"I bet he had medical help," Derek said, standing in the middle of the room.

"Not what I heard," Kelly chimed again.

"He did fuck her ass," I said. "Twice!"

"No way," Derek said.

"That's what I heard," Kelly nodded.

"I have the video proof and the sounds to prove it," I nodded again as I found the contract. I printed it and then handed it to Derek. "Here," I said.

"Nice!" Derek nodded as he looked it over. "Two more houses, then they can ask for a raise, very nice! They will be pissed when they see this," he nodded as he tucked it away.

"If they want to break it, remind them of the penalty," I said, shooing him away.

Derek took one last look at Kelly and then walked out of the office.

"So, what did you hear?" I asked.

"Well, let's just say that conversation lasts longer than he does," Kelly smiled.

I laughed as we continued our talks. It was good to feel normal for a while, but deep down, I was nervous. I knew Benjamin would be building a case for himself.

If he wanted to keep himself in the running for political office, he knew he had to make me out to be the lousy housewife and for him to be the victim.

I had to be ready for anything he would throw at me.

Chapter Three: More Lies

Two more days until the big event and Benjamin's name had been dragged through the mud, he had just won a high-profile case that went nationwide a few months ago, and then he was running for political office on a family-first, tradition-based platform, only for the video of his cheating to go public.

The mayor had already come out a few days ago and rescinded his backing of Benjamin, calling it appalling and against the principles of his new campaign.

Benjamin had yet to leave his hotel room downtown for days as news reporters haggled to get a single word from him.

They were also at my doorstep and workplace, wanting interviews and stories. All I told them was that everything they needed to know was in the video I put out, and other than that, I had no comment.

Charlize ran with it. She was on cloud nine with the fame and pictures all over the internet. She ignored the people that called her names or sent her horrible letters and threats. All she wanted was her name up in the lights.

Sheila came by the other night to tell me that Charlize had already been offered a high-paying porn job and photo opportunities. I was glad I had just made this woman's new career in porn.

Then Charlize made the biggest splash last night. She went on an interview online and revealed that it wasn't just herself, that there were others, other friends of hers, that had slept with other high-profile members of our so-called community, including Stuart. She didn't reveal her friends' names. But she did say there would be more video releases.

I cringed at the thought of what was going to happen next. "What had I started?" I asked myself.

"Not your fault mom," Sheila said as she met me for breakfast. "These people did it to themselves," she tried to reassure me.

I knew this was my doing deep down that I had started the ball rolling down the hill, and now it was just a matter of time before it got out of control.

Reporters were everywhere trying to get their hands on the following videos of politicians, lawyers, and law enforcement leaders, which Charlize had said were part of a vast web of cheating and lies.

Of course, it was all over the talk radio, some of them saying it was all a hoax to bring down the chain of government and slandering people's names.

I wasn't slandering Benjamin's name; he had said many bad things about me on that video. None of it he could take back with an apology or money. He deserved what was coming to him. I didn't feel bad for any of the others. I only felt bad for their wives and their families.

"I have to get in front of this," I nodded.

"What are you going to do?" Sheila asked.

"I have to talk to him," I nodded.

I knew it was a long shot, but if there was any saving grace in this matter, I knew I had to tell Benjamin, to tell the truth about everything, and kill it before it got the chance to be too big. Sure, it would bring down some of his friends, but if it came from him, it would be better than the alternative.

"No way!" Benjamin yelled at me as I tried to talk to him over the phone. "Do you know how far this goes?"

"I have an idea," I replied. "Charlize told Sheila about your little boys club downtown," I said. "How all of you sit down with cigars and drinks while girls dance around in skimpy clothes, while you guys talk about...."

"Fuck, that stupid little bitch!" Benjamin yelled. "She's going to get herself in trouble she can't get out of," Benjamin said.

"Yes, Ben go ahead and threaten a twenty-year old," I shook my head. "Anything happens to her, her friends or her family it will be on the news before you could bat your eyes, then it will get really out of control."

"I wouldn't do that, but there are some others that would take that risk," Benjamin said.

"Let them, but you have to get out before it swallows you up," I pleaded. "If you go...."

"Alison, I can't," Benjamin said as he hung up.

I shook my head as I looked at Sheila. "Any luck with Charlize?" I asked.

"Nope the stupid bitch intends on releasing a video today of the boys club, supposedly Nadine has had it for months," Sheila said, sitting back in her chair.

"Call your siblings, I want them all here," I nodded.

I knew the shit was about to hit the fan and hard.

I CALLED CHARLIZE AND told her to meet me at my house once everyone had come. I thought maybe I could beg her to drop all of this. She seemed like a reasonable person the first time we talked.

"You started this Alison," Charlize said as she sat in my living room. "Benjamin said you would walk away with his offer, if anything happened, but you put out that video for all to see, why shouldn't I?"

"Because it was just you and him," I shook my head.

"How did you get started with all of this anyway?" Dawson asked.

They had all come as quickly as they could. Even my grandkids were here, not at the house at the moment. They were out and about doing fun things.

"I got invited to a party," Charlize shrugged. "One thing led to another and the next day I got invited to show up downtown, was told it would be fun, a few drinks with some people that would help my dancing career, and maybe meet a few people in the business."

Of course, it was to rope her in.

"It was a bunch of old men, sitting at this closed club, well it looked closed from the outside, but inside, it looked brand new," Charlize smiled. "There were tons of other girls dancing on poles and drinks were flowing as well as other things, and that's where I met Ben."

"So, this place, is it still there?" Sheila asked.

"No, they move it, from time to time. It would always be in a different spot, sometimes we would go back to a location, but it was never the same place twice in a row," Nadine said.

Nadine and a few other girls had come along. We were taping it for their security. The questions were relentless as my children got all the information; they could get out of them.

When all was said and done, the truth was all out too bare. I knew only one person could release this video and not face significant consequences.

"JESUS, ALISON," ALEXANDER said as he watched the video for the second time. "You know what this could do?"

I met him in a hotel room on the city's outskirts. "You are friends with most of these guys," I said as I tried to reason with him. "So far, they have done nothing illegal...."

"Illegal? Ha," Alexander laughed. "Most of these men have very high-paying jobs in the foundation of this city. They are cheating with women half their wives' ages. Who knows what else they are doing in that club!"

"You knew about this club?" I asked.

Alexander looked at me with a look that made me instantly regret that question. "Don't you dare lump me up with those fucking idiots. Of course I knew about it, half the city knows about it, why do you think it moves around so much? Those girls should have kept their mouths shut!"

"What's going to happen?" I asked.

"You think this is the first time something like this comes out?" Alexander smiled. "Oh, of course at first there will be chaos, names called out, bridges burned, new elections, but as usual some new scandal will come out, and it will be water under the bridge, as usual, the club will continue with new members, new locations." Alexander nodded.

"The girls?" I asked.

"Tell them to meet me here. I got a few places I can hide them, until the dust settles," Alexander nodded as he handed me a piece of paper with an address on it.

Alexander's family roots went deep in this city; the rumors were rampant. How his family had helped build this city, to some of his family being in the mob, the list went on and on. Alexander never ran for anything political he was happy with his many contacts and businesses around the ever-growing city.

"Don't worry, once people see they are with me, they won't dare do anything to them," Alexander nodded his silver-haired face.

The other rumor was that Alexander ran an underground crime family; I couldn't count how often the FBI or some other group would come and ransack our papers looking for something.

One of the many reasons I liked working for him was the excitement behind it.

Alexander would always say it was because he knew certain people that shouldn't be named. I always laughed at him as he said it, as he always made it sound more prominent than it was, or smaller, whatever needed to be told to put us all at ease.

"Go home Alison, take care of everything else, I will take care of this," Alexander nodded.

"Thank you, Alex," I said as I left.

I stopped at Benjamin's hotel on the way home. I wanted to see him. I didn't know why, but I thought it would be right.

"One last look, huh?" Benjamin asked as he opened the door.

"It's all over," I said as I told him what I knew after sitting across from him.

"The final nail in the coffin," Benjamin nodded. "He's right though," Benjamin said as he poured himself a glass.

"This will be a huge scandal for a few weeks, maybe less. Then something new will pop up, and it would be like nothing happened," Benjamin said. "I was so close," he said, slumping back in his chair.

"You will still be remembered as ...." I started to say.

"As what the lawyer that won a few high-profile cases," Benjamin laughed. "No, this, right here, will be my legacy; this is how I will be remembered," he said.

"You could leave the city. Start over, forge a new path, be remembered elsewhere," I smiled. "There are plenty of places out there that haven't heard of you, or care what you have done, hell even places that need a good lawyer."

Benjamin looked at me. "A fresh start for both of us?"

"No," I shook my head. "That ship sailed the moment you decided I was too boring, and you needed a young mistress," I smiled.

"We had a good run though, right? The first few years?" Benjamin asked.

"Definitely," I nodded. "See you around." I said as I got up and left.

While I was in the elevator, I remembered those first years. We were inseparable, always wanted to be around each other, and always touching and showing each other our affection, even in the most public of places.

Things in the bedroom were just as crazy. We would go days in and out of the bedroom, not wanting to leave the bed or any of the many places we would end up fucking each other's brains out.

I didn't know when exactly things started to fizzle out, maybe after Debra was born, but I knew the fire in the bedroom had died down to embers by the time Sheila came around.

Sheila was conceived while we were on vacation, and that nearly never happened due to Benjamin's workaholic attitude.

Now it was finally over, and by the sounds of things, Benjamin was in no shape to argue.

I HATED ADMITTING TO Alexander that he was right, but I had to do it in the end. He was right about things blowing over.

Two months after the divorce, things were back to normal. During the event, reporters were everywhere, trying to catch glimpses of the cheaters splashed over the news headlines.

Now there was a new national scandal, and no one cared about anything to do with it or the events leading up to it.

I had gotten everything I wanted and didn't take anything extra. I sold the house and then used most of the money to buy a new car and a smaller home.

It was a lovely house with more than enough room just for me, the car was something I had an eye on for a while, and now with the extra money, I decided that I could splurge just a little.

I spread the money among the children, especially Debra and her husband, as they had hit tight monetary problems. Of course, they said they would pay me back, but I wasn't interested. I just wanted to help them out.

The only good thing to come out of everything was the new friends that I had gotten; some of the other wives and I had formed a sort of club just for us. We met every week and did things together.

Tonight, we were having a sort of adult-themed wine party. And things were getting out of hand as usual.

"Stop it," I said as Jacquelyn took one of the gel dildos and put it in her mouth.

"There is no way," Teresa shook her head.

Sure enough, Jacquelyn was deepthroating this eleven-inch marvel. I could see her throat swell as she continued to take it down her throat.

The deal was if she took the whole thing down her throat, I would have to buy one.

"Seriously, stop," I said with a wine glass in my hand, staring at this fifty-three-year-old woman deepthroating an adult toy like it was nothing.

"Here you go," Sheila said.

Sheila was hosting the event at her apartment; she had gone into selling these toys as a part-time job.

I nodded my defeat as Jacquelyn completed her challenge. I swiped my card into the mobile machine to take ownership of one of the gel dildos. I had no idea what I was going to do with it. There was no way I could use it or try anything as Jacquelyn had done.

"What color?" Sheila asked as she showed me a variety of boxes.

"The black one," Jacquelyn said as she grabbed the box and threw it onto my lap.

"Why not," I shrugged after taking the rest of the wine down.

That's how things were with the five of us, we once went to a strip club, and the rest of the girls had the poor male strippers trying to get away from us.

By the night's end, I went home with more adult toys than I had ever purchased. There were suctions, long ones, short vibrating ones. Who knew there were so many toys to get females off?

"Shit," I yelled as I looked in the rear-view mirror and saw the lights of the police officer.

My new car was a sports model. "I should have gotten the V6 model," I said as I pulled over.

I had splurged and got the complete eighty thousand package instead of the fifty. Mine was, of course, fully decked out with all the bells and whistles, but the driver behind the wheel still caused the most problems. One of them being that I had a lead foot.

I saw him slowly walking up to my car when I realized I still had all the adult toys spread across my back seat. Sheila ran out of black bags to put things in, so she threw them into the back.

Then I remembered how much I had to drink and knew I reeked of wine.

"Sorry," I said as he came into view.

"Seventy in a forty-five," he said as he looked at me.

"I am still getting used to it, just bought it a few weeks ago," I nodded as I handed over all the information.

"Had a bit of a party?" he asked as he looked in the back.

"Yes, my daughter threw a party, and it was adult themed," I nodded.

"Drinking?" he asked.

"Just a bit, not too much," I nodded.

I was trying to bluff my way out of an even heftier ticket or worse.

"Let me run all of this, and I will right back with you," he said as he walked away.

I was so screwed. I thought to myself as I tried to relax.

The officer eventually returned with everything, as well as a ticket. "I dropped it to sixty in a fifty-five, but you need to watch your speed, even if it's a new car," he said as he stared at me.

I signed the paper, and he told me all I needed to know about paying it and how not to accumulate even more points; then, he let me go.

I obeyed the speed limit for the rest of the ride home and cursed Sheila for throwing my things into the back so carelessly.

Chapter Four: Moving On

I had to say the single life was starting to feel good. No more thinking of what someone else wanted or what they felt or needed. It was just me. If I wanted to go somewhere, I went. If I wanted something, I got it. It was complete freedom to do what I wanted when I wanted to do it.

The other wives and I were as close to best friends as possible. I could never have had a friendship like this while I was Benjamin. He was always looking at and judging my friends.

"Don't try to hide it," Sheila said as we sat down for our weekly dinner.

"I don't know what you are talking about," I smiled.

"You enjoyed the party last week," Sheila smiled back. "Don't try and say you didn't."

I couldn't. I thought I wouldn't like an adult-themed party with just women, but it was fun to let loose.

"I bet you enjoyed the toys just as much," Sheila said without batting an eye.

"Sheila!" I said, as many people were sitting around our table. We were at our restaurant downtown.

"Tell me I am wrong," Sheila laughed.

I just shook my head. Benjamin had taken my advice and left. He didn't tell me where he was going or what he would do. All I got was a farewell text that was his way of ending everything we had, and I was more than willing to let everything go.

"They don't compare to the real thing," I stated.

I had tried out all of the toys I had gotten that night, and except for the one I sometimes used in the shower that could suction to the wall so I could bounce back on it, all the others did nothing for me.

"Well, you should take that police officer up on his offer," Sheila shrugged.

I told her about the two run-ins with the police officer who frequently patrolled the road leading to my development. The first time he helped me; the second time, he nearly threw the book at me; and the third, he asked if I was trying to get his attention.

None of the times had anything to do with him. I loved speeding in my new car. I barely had to press the gas pedal, and it was shooting past 60mph.

The thought had crossed my mind. Nearly a year without male contact was pushing it for me. I knew they said a woman hit their prime sexual peak in their forties, but I was still peaking, and toys of any nature didn't satisfy the urge.

"I might just do that," I said without thinking.

"Mom, I was joking!" Sheila said.

"Well, it's been a while, and I have needs," I laughed back at her.

I knew I had caught Sheila off guard. She hadn't expected that from her conservative mother.

Usually, I kept that side of me hemmed inside and only let it out in the bedroom, but something pushed me to be more aggressive.

That feeling followed me throughout the day and into most of the afternoon. It wasn't until I was heading home that I decided to act on it.

As I was driving home, I saw the familiar silver and green on the side of the road up ahead, and I punched the gas pedal, sending the speedometer way past eighty.

The familiar sound of the officer chirping his horn and flashing his lights filled my ears and eyes as I looked back.

I waited until he came close to the door. I unbuttoned some buttons on my top and pulled it slightly open, just enough to show I was sporting more than the average-sized chest.

"Now, that was to get my attention," Henry said as he approached my window.

"Absolutely," I nodded.

Henry's eyes fell directly to my chest. Having large breasts usually did that to most men. I was glad to see that being a woman of my age. I hadn't lost my touch.

"Next time, keep the speed down," Henry said as he dropped a card onto my lap.

"Of course, officer," I nodded.

Henry walked away, and I proceeded to do the speed limit the rest of the way home. Once I got home, I texted the number on the card.

'Sorry, if I got you into trouble.'

'No, trouble, just caught me by surprise.'

'Well, I hope it was a good surprise, wouldn't want to disappoint,' I knew I was flirting with a cop, and I didn't even know if he was married or not, something told me he wasn't, but you never know these days.

'You could say it was more than good,' Henry replied.

'Oh, really? Was it me that surprised you or something else?'

There was a moment of silence as I didn't get a response back. I thought I had pushed too far.

'How about I answer that at dinner, tonight?'

I was floored. I hadn't been on a date in forever. Benjamin and I had stopped going on dinner dates a long time ago. I didn't know how to respond for a few minutes; I just looked at the screen.

'Well, you wanted my attention,' Henry added.

'Yes, dinner, tonight,' I responded.

'Good, I will pick you up at eight,' Henry said.

'No,' I said; part of me still wanted to be the new independent woman I had become. *'Send me the address and I will meet you there.'*

'Will do,' Henry replied. 'See you tonight.'

I had time before the night's event, so I decided to clean. It was something I did when I was nervous about anything. And now I was nervous about going on a date with a guy I hardly knew.

My only involvement with Henry was through my newfound need for speed.

I couldn't believe I had agreed to meet him. He was a cop, and I still didn't know his age. What did he like? If he was married? Had he been married? The more I thought about it, the more I wanted to pick up my phone and call it off.

Just as I was about to call it off and settle in for the night, I got a video call from Debra. We talked about many things, most of which involved my grandchildren and the times that I would see them, but then she mentioned a few problems that she was having with her health. Before I knew it, the time had flown by, and I was nearing meeting Henry.

"Mom?" Debra asked as she saw me peering at the clock behind me. "Do you have a date?"

"What, no, I mean, it's okay," I said as I felt flustered.

"Go, you haven't been on one since, well before all of us were born," Debra smiled back at me.

"I don't know anything about him," I said.

"Staying home, won't help that, now, will it?" Debra said as she shook her head. "Go, have fun!"

I finally agreed with what Debra was saying. I needed to get out there. Even though I had been going out with friends, it would be nice to go out again and pursue a relationship.

HENRY'S EYES WENT WIDE as he saw me walking toward him. I had dressed semi-casually as the place seemed like a regular steak restaurant.

"Well?" I asked. "Is it something I said?"

"No, not at all," Henry said. He was still staring at me. "I just didn't think you would be so, stunning."

"Good choice of words," I said as I walked inside.

The date was going fine. I learned a lot about Henry. He used to work in security and then decided to join the police force. He wasn't currently married, and he was only two years older than me and was soon retiring from the workforce.

I told him about myself, and he said he knew everything about me. After he stopped me the second time, he decided to look more into me. Finding out about my divorce and Benjamin and all the others, he got more intrigued.

I had to admit that I was having a good time talking to someone other than my children and the female friends I had thought of as sisters. Henry was a welcome change of pace.

Of course, the other thing I missed was the occasional stare at my cleavage. Henry tried to play it off by looking elsewhere when I caught him, but I knew he was looking, and I liked the attention.

After dinner, we walked into the old part of downtown. It was a nice chilly night, not too cold or windy for a change. We talked more about things we had interests in. He wanted to leave the big city, go out to the country, buy a house on an extensive stretch of land, and disappear.

That sounded nice, but I always had been a city gal. I loved the noises and the bright lights. Sure, my house was outside the big city but not too far. I could still see the tall buildings from my bedroom window.

I told him about eventually starting my own real estate company or a small diner. I loved to cook. It was how most of my children got as big as they were, he wanted to meet them all eventually, but I told him they were all grown up and had lives of their own.

"This was nice," Henry said as we made a full circle back to the restaurant.

"Very," I said as I looked up at him.

Henry was slightly taller than me, not too tall. His black hair had grey, and his beard was salt and peppered. He looked down at me through those steel-blue eyes. I knew he wanted to kiss me, and I wanted him to, so I leaned forward and let him.

I loved being held tightly, and Henry held me tight against him as he kissed me. It wasn't the best of kisses. I am sure we were both out of practice. After we kissed, we lingered for a while, staring at each other. His strong hands were around my waist and just above my ass.

"I think we should call it a night," I said as I pushed off him.

"You're right," Henry said.

Henry followed me to my car, and then we said our goodbyes.

I felt the usual afterglow of a good date on the drive home, and I wanted no more than to see Henry again.

When I got home, I texted Henry to let him know I was home safely. He replied quickly, letting me know he was also home.

That's when he called me. We spoke for hours, way into the night and the early morning.

"HOW DID IT GO?" ONE of my friends asked as I met her for lunch.

I smiled as I remembered the night. "It was memorable," I replied.

"Oh yeah," Sabrina said. "That memorable, huh?" she smiled.

"No, nothing like that," I shook my head.

"Uh huh," Sabrina nodded. "I am sure he was thinking about it."

I nodded. From our talk later that night, I knew Henry was interested in me in more ways than just talking. As a typical male, he asked the usual questions about what I was into, and I was not ashamed to answer them.

After all, I was a very sexual person when the time came, and I was sure Henry would find out about that firsthand sooner than he thought. After all, I wanted what he wanted.

"Oh no," Sabrina smiled. "I know that look."

"There is no look," I said, shaking my head.

"Poor guy doesn't know what he is in for," Sabrina smiled.

After lunch, I returned to work, and my thoughts dwelled on tonight's meeting with Henry. It was my time to pick where we would be going. I knew of a perfect spot. It was secluded and had excellent music. I went there a long time ago with some potential buyers. It would be perfect for a second date.

I met Henry later that night, and as usual, he had his eyes on me the moment I stepped out of the car. "If you keep that up, your eyes will fall out of your head."

"I can't help it, you always look so stunning," Henry smiled as he took my hand as we walked inside.

Henry was a perfect gentleman, always opening the door and ensuring I got seated first. He even tried to pick up the tab this time, which I fought for, and eventually, he caved.

I was sure he would get his way the next time, but tonight was my turn, and I wouldn't give it up.

We danced at another place down the road from the restaurant, and I had to admit to Henry he was a much better dancer than Benjamin ever was. He took that as a compliment.

The night got late, and we were both getting tired, but at the same time, we didn't want to leave each other's side.

As he walked me back to my car, he pulled me close to him. "You sure you want to go home?" Henry asked.

I knew I should say yes. Every part of me that was a good woman wanted to say yes and go back home, but the more significant part wanted to see where this night would lead.

I knew where Henry's mind wanted to go. He had stolen glances at my cleavage during the night and many times. His hands wandered over my body during the dances. If I had to guess, Henry was an ass man. His hands had grabbed mine many times tonight.

"No," I replied in a whisper. "I don't."

'Traitor!' my inner voice yelled.

"Follow me," Henry said as he got in his car.

I followed him through the streets of downtown into the parking garage of an expensive hotel.

"You devil!" I said, as Henry already had a room booked.

"What can I say after last night's talk, I thought I would shoot my shot," Henry said as we got in the elevator.

"Well, your aim is good, let's see what else," I flirted as I kissed him.

Now it was time for my hands to wander. I grabbed his groin and was pleased to feel that Henry was already semi-hard. He was no Benjamin, but at least it was the real thing and not a toy.

"Alison," Benjamin growled in a low voice as I held and massaged his growing cock.

"Yes?" I answered as I looked up at him.

"Got two more floors, to go," Henry said, breathing heavily.

I had his dick at full mast in my hand, and I could tell he was putty in my hands, literally.

As the door to the elevator opened, Henry tried to walk correctly with a hard cock between his legs. I had to smile as I walked beside him.

"You haven't seen anything yet," I warned him as he opened the door.

We quickly rushed inside, and before he closed it, I was already on my knees. Seconds later, I had his white cock in my mouth. Benjamin was a lot longer and thicker, so taking Henry's cock in my mouth was an easy accomplishment.

"Holy fuck," Henry said as he stood in the hallway with his back against the wall.

'Not already,' I thought to myself. I hadn't even started yet.

I slowly eased off and slowed down, but it was too late. The floodgates had opened.

Henry came hard as he filled my mouth. His hands gripped my head tightly as he thrust his cock into my mouth. It hadn't been three minutes since we entered the hotel room.

"Fuck!" Henry exclaimed as he finished.

'Typical,' I thought as Henry started to walk away, with me still on my knees.

"Well," I said as I got up.

"No, sorry," Henry said as he walked me to the large living room.

"I am used to it," I nodded.

"It's just been so long since the last time and..." Henry explained.

"No, it's okay, hopefully the rest of the night will be better," I said.

As the saying goes, these are famous last words.

After a short break, Henry and I went to the bedroom, where things got progressively worse. First, Henry tried to go down on me, which was a feeble attempt. He mostly used his fingers and, for the most part, fumbled around as if he was in a hurry.

Then when we finally got down to having sex, he lasted two minutes both times. Of course, he blamed it on not being with a woman for four years. Which I thought was a good excuse for the first night.

I REALIZED HENRY'S shortness in the bedroom would become a recurring theme after our third night in bed together. I had tried everything a woman could do to help a man with that problem.

I had tried to be on top, which was a mistake as he came even faster; the sight of my big boobs bouncing all over the place made him cum in less than a minute. Then I tried not to have any type of foreplay, which I hated, but it led to the same result.

The moment Henry entered me, I could count how long it would take him to cum. He made the same faces, and seconds later, he would roll over onto his side with some apology.

When I brought it up, he always had an excuse. Until I decided that he would have to start wearing protection, that was when things got hairy.

After another disappointing short burst of sex, I decided I had enough and brought up the idea of him using protection. It was something that I had thought about for a while.

I loved everything else about Henry. He was charming, a gentleman. He made me laugh and always cared about me and what I was doing, unlike Benjamin, who wouldn't listen when I tried to tell him about my day. Henry would listen and offer insight. He even came to see one of my house showings.

But in the bedroom, he was lacking, which was causing problems. I tried to get him to use toys with me so that we could both enjoy the experience, but he didn't want to do that because it made him feel inferior.

"I don't know what you want from me," Henry said when I brought it up.

"If you don't know, that's half the problem," I replied as I got out of bed.

"Janice never had a problem," Henry said, shaking his head.

'Yes, bring up your ex-wife while your girlfriend is trying to talk to you because that always works!" I yelled. "By the way, Janice left you and is fucking another woman! Newsflash! She had a problem!"

That lit a fire. I could see the look on Henry's face. He was beyond pissed.

"Take it back!" Henry shouted. "Right now!"

"No," I said as I started to put on my clothes. "Janice was the one that wanted the divorce, right? She was even the one that got all the papers started. You didn't find it odd that she left the county when the ink dried. Or that she started seeing women?"

"Alison, stop talking right now!" Henry said, shaking his head.

"Janice is right now in bed with another woman, that get this, looks like a man!" I shouted back at him. "I've seen the pictures. Her girlfriend looks like a man! I bet you she doesn't have to go back home to get herself off."

"Leave!" Henry shouted as he pointed to the bedroom door.

"For a cop, you really aren't bright," I said as I put on my shoes. "I'm already dressed! Where do you think I am going?"

Henry slammed the door behind me as I left. I walked to my car and slammed the door shut. I screamed as I started the car.

If this was how dating was going to be, I would rather be single.

Chapter Five: Getting Over It

IT HAD BEEN TWO WEEKS since the breakup with Henry, and we had no contact with each other. I drowned myself in my work and tried to forget about him, but it was more challenging than it seemed.

It was becoming clear that I wasn't ready to return to the dating world. I blamed myself for the problems with Henry, he was a good man, and I tore him down because he wasn't good in bed.

All kinds of thoughts filled my head. Maybe I could have ignored it. Perhaps I went too far.

I sat down with my friends and asked if they had encountered the same problems. Since they, too, had gone through the same thing as I had.

"He's a man," Jacquelyn shrugged. "Nathan was the same way at the beginning."

Jacquelyn, the most outgoing of all of us, had been married to a police commissioner before everything went down. Now, she was happily divorced and seeing her neighbor.

"But's he's, well you know," Sabrina said.

"No, I don't," Jacquelyn shook her head. She was teasing Sabrina, who was more introverted than the rest of us.

"Black," Sabrina whispered.

"Sweetie, the nearest table is nowhere near listening range," Francis shook her head. "You don't need to whisper."

"What's the color of his skin have to do with sex?" Jaquelyn asked. "Unless you're one of those simpletons that believe the internet and stupid rumors?"

"Well, some rumors are based on facts," Cassandra noted.

Cassandra and Francis were in the same boat as Jaquelyn and me. They were once married to high-ranking officials caught in the scandal, and both were divorced.

Cassandra quickly remarried one of her coworkers, and Francis was like me, single and looking. On the other hand, Sabrina was one of the few women that knew about the club and were paid to keep it hushed.

"Some," Jaquelyn nodded. "I've dated a few men in my time."

"A few?" Francis smirked.

"Okay, a lot," Jaquelyn smiled. "Let me tell you something, color of their skin or prowess on any field of sport has nothing to do with their abilities in the bedroom."

"Amen," Cassandra nodded as the two clinked their wine glasses. Sabrina nodded.

"So, I should have accepted it and moved on?" I asked.

"You said he was a good man outside of the bedroom?" Francis asked.

"Yes, very," I nodded.

"Take it and run," Jaquelyn nodded at me. "Take it and run for the hills, lock that man in a vault and plaster your name all over it."

Cassandra was the only one shaking her head. "Not me," she said as she sat back. "Did that with my first marriage and look what that got me?"

The others stopped drinking.

"For all those years I accepted everything he spouted at me. I was a good patient wife, never questioned, never disobeyed," Cassandra shook her head. "I told Timothy before we got married, I wouldn't be that wife again, it's both ways or the highway."

That's how I felt. Now that I had a taste of being alone, I wasn't afraid of being single for a very long time.

"What did he say?" Francis asked.

"He put the ring on my finger, and now I have it both ways. He is an excellent husband and a very patient and understanding lover, not like the other one," Cassandra smiled.

"Well, good," Jaquelyn stated. "Maybe he needs to come over and talk to Nathan," Jaquelyn nodded. "I get a few minutes of entertainment and pfft he is done and over on the other side of the bed snoring."

"Three minutes," I nodded. "Three minutes and he was done."

"Nope," Sabrina shook her head. "I couldn't do it."

"Ladies," Francis shook her head. "Face the truth, men reach their sexual prime in their twenties, and sometimes thirties, after that it's downhill and fast. All of us are in our fifties and in our prime and I am sorry to say unless you all turn into cougars and start dating younger men, this is what you're going to deal with and that's putting it lightly. Men our age don't have the stamina anymore, they just don't, no amount of complaining or pointing it out will change that, and that's just the facts."

The table went silent as usual whenever Francis laid out the facts. She was a medical doctor, and she often laid the hammer down during our talks. Henry was in his mid-fifties. Was I asking too much of him to try and keep up with me?

"That's what the blue pill is for," Jaquelyn laughed as the table returned to its joyous repertoire.

AFTER DINNER, I THOUGHT about it more. While cleaning the old house before I moved, I found some prescriptions for Benjamin hidden in a fake drawer in the bedroom. They were for his libido. I wondered how he kept up with such a young woman; it seemed like he had some medical help.

Maybe I should accept that Henry was right, he couldn't keep up, but that meant I would be unhappy and unsatisfied and leave my pleasure to myself. Then what was the point of having him around then?

"Shit," I said as I turned the corner to my house. "Talk of the devil."

I pulled up and got out of the car. "I thought I had given you enough space to calm down," Henry said as I exited the vehicle.

I sighed and looked at him. "Could have called, or sent a text," I said as I made my way down the driveway toward him.

"Wouldn't have seemed right," Henry shrugged. "I wanted to tell you; I was sorry for yelling at you."

"And?" I asked.

"Bringing up my ex-wife at that time was the wrong thing to do," Henry added.

"Bingo, we could have talked, but that really set me off," I responded.

"I'm sorry, just not used to having that part thrown in my face like that," Henry stated.

"I wasn't attacking your man hood, or anything I was just saying I was unsatisfied, and wanted to talk about it," I said, looking at him.

"Well, when a woman says that it does seem like an attack," Henry said, leaning against his car.

"Well, it's not," I replied. "I would never say you're less than a man, for any reason."

"That's a relief," Henry smiled.

"Come on, let's go inside and talk," I motioned.

We talked for hours over it, and of course, things got a little heated a few times, but I had put my foot down.

I wouldn't take care of things myself if I were with someone. I could do it myself, being single, if that were the case. Henry said he would see a specialist and see about taking medication if it came to that, but he also put his foot down that he wouldn't be using what he called *'play toys'* to help me.

Ultimately, I ended up unsatisfied again that night after another three-minute session. I watched Henry as he slept. Wondering if things would ever change.

"YOU'RE A CUM DUMPSTER!" Sheila laughed as she helped me around the house.

The holidays were coming, and everyone was coming to my new house. "I still hate that Jaquelyn and you talk to each other," I said, shaking my head.

"And I am sorry that you're a cum dumpster, mom," Sheila smiled.

I cringed every time she said those words, but they were accurate. I just wish she didn't repeat them.

"Don't worry, lots of women go through it," Debra said as she had also come to set things up.

"Great, the two of you are agreeing for once," I shook my head.

"It's a topic a lot of women have in common," Debra shrugged.

"Not me," Sheila shook her head. "Grant was like that, and after a few times of him not listening, I kicked him to the curb."

"Grant, the tall basketball player?" Debra asked. "Or was he the swimmer?"

"Funny!" Sheila said.

Debra always picked on her little sister on the number of guys she dated.

"Well, we can't keep track," Debra shrugged.

"Sorry, how long does Jimmy last, and when was the last time, he brought you to an orgasm without the toys you bought from me?" Sheila asked as she stood on a ladder, putting up decorations.

"Low blow and you know it!" Debra shouted at her sister. "He has back problems, and low testosterone."

"That long huh?" Sheila nodded. "Fifteen minutes and twice, and it happened last night. Four separate times."

"Are we going to meet this one, or does he have something more important to do?" Debra asked.

I loved these moments. Even though they went back and forth, they loved each other. Anytime the other was remotely sick or went out of contact for a while, the other was in a total mess. This was just their way of talking to each other.

"I am sorry, I couldn't hear you over the loud, desperate sound of a woman needing a decent orgasm," Sheila said.

This went on for most of the day, but in the end, the outside and interior of the house looked ready for the holidays.

"She's not wrong," Debra said as Sheila got in her car.

Debra was staying at my house until everyone came home the following week.

"You don't have to put up with it, either." I stated.

"I love Jimmy, do you love Henry?" Debra asked. "That's the difference."

'Straight to the heart,' I thought as Debra went upstairs.

She was right. I didn't love Henry. Debra could put up with Jimmy's shortcomings because she loved him, and he loved her enough to ensure she got hers, even if that meant using other means.

"I DON'T. I AM SORRY," Debra said as we were returning home from a lunch date with Henry.

"What about him that you don't like?" I asked.

"That macho man thing he's got going on," Debra shook her head. "He didn't even ask if you wanted the wine he ordered."

"I've drank it before, he knows what I like," I shrugged.

"For dinner," Debra said as she drove. "You never drink that one for lunch. Unless things have dramatically changed."

I shook my head. "It was okay," I shrugged.

"Tenth," Debra said.

"What?" I asked.

"That's the tenth time you have said, it's okay when it comes to things he does," Debra stated.

"You just went into the lunch with a bad idea of him in your head," I shook my head.

"No, not fair," Debra shook her head. "I came to give him a chance, and he blew it, I am sorry, you can do a lot better."

I sat in silence for the rest of the drive.

A few things were going south in my relationship with Henry. Even after going to the specialist and taking medication, things in the bedroom had not changed.

Henry refused to use other means and now was adamant about not going down on me, saying he wasn't good at it and it wasn't something that needed to be done.

I then told him I wouldn't do it for him, which caused an even bigger argument. Even when I put his cock between my tits, and tit fucked him, he lasted even shorter.

It was a whole week since we hadn't had sex, and I was already dreading the next time. Debra was right about one thing. I had said it's okay for many things. Maybe I was wrong about not being afraid to be alone.

"He's still coming to the dinner Sunday?" Debra asked.

"Yeah," I nodded.

"You will see, the others will think the same," Debra stated.

I hoped not. I was trying to make this relationship work, but if Debra was right and I was the only one trying, what was the use?

CHRISTMAS DINNER WAS a big deal in our family, and the table was filled with lots of food. The grandchildren were out in my backyard throwing snow everywhere.

The smell of Christmas flowed through the house, and even though it was my first Christmas without Benjamin, I still wished him a good time wherever he was; Henry was late, and it wasn't going well with the clan.

I made Debra and Sheila promise not to tell the others about our problems. They promised not to be the first ones to bring it up.

There was a knock on the door, and Mason quickly got up and got it. My heart was beating out of my chest. Mason was very protective of his mother, and I was sure he was ready to pounce if things went wrong.

"Sorry, traffic with the snow is a bear out there," Henry said as he entered.

"We had no problems coming from the airport," Pamela stated. Unlike her husband, Dawson, Pamela spoke her mind; she always said they forgot to install a filter when she was born.

Jimmy and the kids came in from outside, and instantly all of the kids stopped when they saw Henry.

"They are like that with strangers," Jimmy smiled.

Jimmy was the kind person in our family. He never met a stranger that wasn't a potential friend. Jimmy walked from the kitchen's back door to the front of the house.

"Jimmy Gray," Jimmy stated.

"He knows who you are, Jimmy," Debra smiled as she took her husband away. "Come on, let's get all that snow off all of you, so we can have dinner," she said as she got the children and took them upstairs.

I went around the room introducing everyone. It didn't take long for the questions to come in, hot and heavy. Dawson was the one that surprised me. He had many questions about laws and enforcement. Something Henry wasn't happy about; I could tell by the looks he gave Dawson.

"WELL, THAT WENT WELL," Henry stated as we watched everyone leave after dinner.

It didn't go well at all. There was a lot of silence at the table during dinner. A small argument broke out between Mason and Henry after Henry mentioned Dawson's weight.

"They don't like me, do they?" Henry smiled.

I shook my head. None of them did, which was terrible. They hardly ever agreed with anything. Especially Pamela and Jimmy. They were always at opposite ends of the spectrum, but tonight I could see they both agreed.

"Well at least the youngest grandchild liked me," Henry said as he tried to break the silence that had befallen me.

"Taylor," I nodded. "She likes tall men for some reason," but I knew it was because he was tall and reminded her of that superhero she met at Disney.

"I am sorry, I know this was a big deal for you," Henry said as we walked inside.

"Do you have to be a cop even when off duty?" I asked as the door closed.

"Dawson has to realize we enforce the rules. We don't make them up," Henry stated.

"Dawson went to law school and passed. He knows the laws. He knows what he is talking about; he's very smart," I stated.

"And very large," Henry added.

"Yes, because again bringing that up, went very well with Mason," I shook my head.

"Mason is a bag of testosterone; he is going to get himself thrown in jail or worse with that attitude!" Henry shouted.

"What about Jimmy, he was nothing but nice to you all night," I said.

"His wife was catering to all his needs! He was like a grown child!" Henry shouted.

"He had an accident at work, he has had four back surgeries!" I shouted back at him. "He loves his wife and his children, and for the record from what Debra says, none of those back problems stops him from performing in the bedroom!"

"Here we go, right back full circle," Henry said as he picked up his things. "Now I know why Benjamin cheated on you. He couldn't please the ice queen!"

"Oh, he did that and more! The reason he cheated was because I didn't bow down to him, and I won't bow to you," I shouted back.

Henry shook his head. "Watch your speeding from now on. I won't be so nice," he said as he left.

That was it, the last straw. There was no going back this time. I sat down at the table and called Jaquelyn.

"Hi, sorry to bother you on the holidays, but can you come over?" I asked.

"Be right there," Jaquelyn said.

Jaquelyn helped me clean up the family dinner mess and ensured I was alright. She wasn't alone, as she had called the others.

"Well, he will be off that patrol, tomorrow," Sabrina stated as she got off the phone.

"You didn't have to," I said.

"Yes, she did," Francis nodded. "He threatened you. It's an open stretch of road. If you speed, he has to obey the law just like every other cop. He would have been gunning for you every time you went a mile over the speed limit."

Jaquelyn nodded. She was silent for a change, and I was sure she felt guilty for talking me into going back to him.

"Dammit," I said, looking at the table. "He forgot his watch; he took it off to show Taylor...."

"I know someone that can get it to him," Jaquelyn said as she picked it up.

"You will have someone looking over the house tonight and tomorrow," Sabrina said as she got off the phone again.

"How many people in the mayor's office do you know?" Cassandra smiled.

"Enough," Sabrina smiled.

"Again, I don't think he will be back," I nodded.

"His ex-wife filed for a restraining order for a reason," Jaquelyn said.

"Wish I knew that about him beforehand," I said.

"You sure you don't want to call your kids back?" Jaquelyn asked as they all started to leave.

It was getting late, and I knew they would all be getting some sleep before their flights back home tomorrow.

"No, Sabrina's friend is parked right there," I said, looking at the patrol car outside my house.

"Call us, and make sure you keep it handy, just in case," Jaquelyn said as she looked at my drawer where I kept my gun.

"Doubt it will come to that, but I will," I nodded.

"Sorry again for...." Jaquelyn said.

"I was the one that made up the excuses for him. This is on me," I nodded.

The house fell silent as I made my way upstairs to my room. I ensured all the doors were locked and the alarm system was armed. I took Jaquelyn's advice and slept with it under my pillow for the first time.

I couldn't get over the look on Henry's face as he stormed out. It scared me.

'I heard what happened,' a text came over my phone. *'Need ANYTHING from me?'*

It was Alexander. I didn't know how he had found out, but I wasn't surprised. I reread it and at the word anything and how it was all in caps.

Something told me he didn't mean the usual anything. I knew Henry was mad, but I didn't want Alexander to be involved.

'No, I am good, for now,' I typed back. *'If ANYTHING comes up, I will let you know.'*

'Here if you need me,' Alexander responded.

For some reason, I felt better, like there was a safety net around me. Slowly I fell asleep.

Chapter Six: Being Alone

It took a couple of months for things to die down completely. The first week Henry filled my texts and calls, blaming me for his apparent 'demotion' as he put it, as he was taken off his regular patrol and put somewhere else.

Then after I blocked him, he started to come by unannounced, never as far as coming inside or approaching me, but I always saw his car driving by my workplace or by a house I was trying to sell. It would always roll by or stay parked until I noticed, then speed off.

Alexander often asked if I wanted him to take care of it, but I knew it would die down. Henry was just mad, and this was his way of venting.

Finally, it took me storming over to his house to get things settled.

I told him it was over, and no matter how much 'space' he was going to give me or 'attention' he wanted to get, I wasn't coming back to him.

It took a few more days to get through to him, but eventually, the stalking stopped. I hoped that he had found something new to fill his time. I hoped it wasn't someone else as I didn't want Henry to fool someone else with his pretense of being a nice guy and then turn on them the way he did with me.

The new cop on the stretch pulled me over just once when I was way above the speed limit. He gave me a warning and then apologized for what I went through with Henry. It seemed Henry had a reputation of going off on some of the younger officers.

"I am sorry, it's just this open road and my foot seems to want to...." I started to say as he gave me the warning.

"Set your GPS to give you a chirp once you go over the speed limit," the officer said, pointing at my GPS system. "It should slow you down."

"I didn't know it could do that," I said.

"Sure, may I show you?" the young officer said.

"Absolutely," I nodded.

The officer got in the passenger side and showed me how to set it up. Then he allowed me to speed off. Sure, enough, the loud chirp went off after going five miles per hour over the speed limit.

"Well, that's annoying," I said as he caught up to me as I parked.

"I set it to go off continuously until you go under," he smiled.

"And you're not going to tell me how to turn it back off?" I smiled.

"Nope, have a good day," he smiled back at me.

"Rascal!" I shouted back at him.

It had worked. The annoying chirp got me to drop my speed everywhere I went. It was slowly bringing me used to doing the speed limit. This was a bonus as paying for speeding tickets was becoming a chore.

Things were good for me; finally, there were no problems from Henry, and Debra and Jimmy's health problems were under control.

Mason had found a girlfriend, Debbie. He had brought her to see me a few weeks ago. She was lovely. The best thing about her was she kept him under wraps.

He hardly had an outburst the whole three days they were here. I couldn't hug her hard enough and thank her. She truly knew how to calm him down.

That was the thing about a good relationship. One always countered the other. I wondered if I would ever be in a relationship like that again.

"Should get it tinted," Alexander said one day as he drove with me to one of our new locations.

"I was thinking about it, since summer is coming," I replied.

"I know a guy, he's pretty good, and the price isn't bad," Alexander said.

"Absolutely," I nodded.

I loved my job. It had always been the one thing I could count on to be stable. Even when things went haywire, I knew how to fix it.

"You're kidding," I said as Alexander showed me the guy.

"Nope," Alexander said.

In the same strip mall was a small building with big signs that said tinting and other things.

"How did I not notice that?" I asked.

"You never needed it before," Alexander smiled.

I nodded and couldn't believe that I had wanted to get my car tinted for months and didn't notice the building right in front of my workplace.

I drove my car over and went inside.

"Was wondering when you would come in," a tall black man said.

"Me?" I smiled.

"No, the other white lady behind you," the man smiled.

"Funny," I smiled back at him.

"Andre," the man said, holding out his hand.

"Alison," I smiled back at him.

"So, full tint?" Andre asked.

"Yes, not too dark, I already get pulled over enough," I stated.

"That beauty is meant to be driven fast," Andre said as he came around the counter.

"I have the speeding tickets to attest to that," I smiled as we went outside.

Andre walked around my car. "Rims?"

"Uh, don't think so, just the tint," I said as I followed him.

"Black on black would look good," Andre said.

I thought about it and remembered another car like mine with full black rims and thought mine would look good that way.

"Tell you what let me show you," Andre said.

I stood still and stared at my car as Andre went into the garage portion of his building. He came out rolling a tire with black rims.

"I got other designs, which you can pick from, just giving you an idea," Andre said as he held the tire near my car.

I liked it. I didn't just like it; I loved it. "You said other designs?" I asked.

"Yeah, come inside," Andre smiled.

Andre went over many designs and sizes, and I picked out the one I liked.

"Now, how about that speeding?" Andre smiled.

"Someone set me up with that annoying chirp sound," I shook my head as I thought about it.

Andre shook his head and made the sound. "Yes!" I shouted.

"Here, I got something for you," Andre said as he went to the back and brought out a box. "Radar detection, really small, easy to hide and always accurate, hear the low beep, a cop is around," he smiled.

"Are you trying to get a big sale out of me?" I smiled.

"Nope, this one is for free," Andre smiled back.

"Nothing's for free," I smiled.

"Just keep smiling and I will accept that as payment," Andre said.

I felt myself blushing. "Or you can do that, I accept that as well," Andre smiled.

Again, I couldn't stop myself from laughing. "Stop it," I said, shaking my head.

"That too," Andre smiled.

"Okay, enough," I said, coughing and straightening my face.

We stared at each other for a few seconds before I started smiling again.

"Stop!" I yelled at him.

"Didn't do anything that time," Andre said.

"You were thinking it," I said.

"Alison, if you knew what I was thinking you would slap me," Andre said.

I opened my mouth in shock. "Andre! I am old enough to be your mother!"

"Age is just a number," Andre nodded.

"So, that's how you get the big sales huh? Flirt with all the female customers?" I asked. I found myself leaning on the counter, staring at him.

"Flirting? Me? Never!" Andre said, shaking his head.

"You're doing it right now!" I said.

"Now?"

"Yes!"

"No!"

"Definitely, flirting," I said.

"Okay, maybe a little," Andre smiled as he pushed the small box over to me. "But it's still free."

"A lot and I will take it," I nodded.

"I will let you know when the rims come in and do the tints and everything together," Andre said.

"Sounds good," I nodded. "Shall I leave my number?"

"No, I know where you work," Andre nodded.

"How?" I started to ask but then realized where I was and shook my head. "Don't answer that."

"I will come by when it's all here," Andre smiled.

"Bye Andre," I said as I turned to walk away.

"Hate that you're leaving but love looking at you when you go," Andre said.

"What?" I asked.

"Nothing," Andre said as I walked out the door.

It was easy to install the radar detector, and it even came with a clamp to hide under the seat. "Now only if I knew how to turn the damn chirp off," I said as I sat in my car.

There was a knock on my window. I shook my head with a smile. "Looking for something else to sell me?"

Andre shook his head. "The right button," he said, pointing to my dashboard. I followed his directions and turned the chirp to just one chirp after I went over the speed limit.

"Thank you," I nodded.

"Anytime, now are you staying in my parking lot or you coming back inside for more talking?" Andre asked.

I shook my head and stared at him. "How old are you?" I asked.

"Turning forty, next month," Andre said.

"My two oldest sons are three years younger than you," I said, shaking my head.

"That's good to know, but what has that got to do with you in my parking lot?" Andre smiled.

"You're so bad," I said, turning my car on.

"I take it you're not coming back inside," Andre smiled as he stood up.

"No, I am not," I smiled back at him.

I had the same smile as I walked back into my office and sat down.

"Wow!" Kelly said as she looked over at me.

"What?" I replied.

"Alex, come here for a second," Kelly yelled.

Alexander, who was hardly ever in the office, walked over and looked over at me. "Well, that's new."

"What?" I asked.

"You're smiling," Kelly nodded.

"Glowing more like," Alexander said as the two stared at me.

"I smile," I said as I brushed my hair, it was windy outside.

"And brushing the hair," Alexander stated as he sat on Kelly's desk.

"She hardly ever brushes her hair, even on the windy days," Kelly said, shaking her head.

"It's very windy outside," I said.

"Still smiling too," Alexander added.

"Enough," I said, putting the brush down.

"She's trying to be serious with a smile on her face," Kelly said. "Who is he?"

"No one," I said, shaking my head.

"I have known you for years and never seen that smile on your face, except when Mason didn't have to go to jail for hitting that guy," Alexander said. "Spill it."

I sighed and shook my head. "It's nothing, it was just funny," I shrugged.

"It?" Kelly asked.

"Andre and I had a little back and forth talk and it was funny, I haven't laughed like that in a while," I shrugged.

"Andre, huh?" Alexander nodded.

"Isn't he the tint guy?" Kelly asked.

"Well, he does more than tints," I added.

"Like making you laugh," Alexander smiled.

"Yes, I mean he was funny," I said. "It's what he does to make sales."

"Didn't make me laugh," Kelly said.

"Me either," Alexander said.

I started smiling again as I remembered more of the conversation. "It looks good on you," Alexander said as he walked back to his office.

"Real good," Kelly smiled.

For the rest of the day, I had a smile on my face.

"HENRY MADE YOU LAUGH," Sabrina said as I met her for lunch later.

"He made me laugh, not smile," I added. "I can't stop."

"I can see that," Sabrina smiled. "What did he say?"

"It wasn't what he said, it's how he said it, and the looks and the smile, and oh, he so good at flirting, but not pushing it over to the creepy side," I said, shaking my head.

"Like?" Sabrina asked.

"He said if I knew what he was thinking I would slap him," I said.

"Wow," Sabrina blushed. "That's a lot of things and nothing."

"Exactly!" I smiled. "Then he said this thing about hating to see me go and loving to watch me leave or something like that?"

"Your ass," another lady at the other table said. "He meant he was staring at your ass."

I almost spilt my drink. I had never heard it put like that. "Sorry, just overheard your conversation, but that's what he meant."

"Thank you," Sabrina nodded.

We both started talking more quietly after that, but to say I was flustered was a small word for how I felt.

I walked back into Andre's place and saw a young woman at the counter.

I waited in line as Andre took payment, then wished her a good day, no flirting, no pickup line, nothing.

As the lady left and Andre looked up at me, he smiled. "No," he said.

"No, what?" I asked as I walked toward the counter.

"You can't have my number," Andre said.

I was floored again. A smile broke my face, and I had sat in my car for a good twenty minutes thinking about all the things I went through in the past year to make myself feel aggravated.

I took a deep breath and straightened my face.

"Oh no, we are going to be serious now," Andre said as he followed suit and took a deep breath. "Yes ma'am, how can I help you today?"

I busted into laughter. "Stop!" I said, shaking my head. "You're so bad at that."

"I don't know what you mean ma'am, how can I assist you today?" Andre said, still holding a straight face.

"Andre! Stop it," I said as I stared at him. "I am older than you and I say stop."

Andre shrugged and smiled. "The customer is always right," he smiled.

"I came to ask you something and I want a serious answer," I said.

"Back to serious, okay," Andre said as he put his serious face back on.

"Were you checking out my ass?" I asked.

"Yes," Andre answered. "Well, which time exactly?"

"There's been more than one time?" I asked, stunned.

"Well, you do work right there," Andre said as he motioned out the window on the left. Outside I could see my office.

"You've been stalking me?" I laughed.

"Stalking, admiring, whichever," Andre shrugged.

"Kelly's much more attractive and she's closer to your age," I said, but deep down, I found it alluring that such a handsome young man was admiring me.

"Honest?" Andre asked.

"Totally," I nodded.

"You're much more attractive than she is, plus," Andre said as he leaned forward over the counter and stared behind me. "She doesn't have that," he said.

"Andre!" I said, pushing him back behind the counter and staring behind me. We were the only ones in the small building.

"You told me to be honest," Andre shrugged.

"How old am I?" I asked.

"Don't care," Andre shrugged.

"Fifty-two," I replied.

"Nope, still don't care," Andre shrugged again.

I couldn't believe it. I was flirting back with him. I was even considering giving him my number.

"Here," Andre said. "That is my card, and that's my cell phone number on the back, if you want you can call or text me."

I took it and held it in my hand. "You're welcome," Andre said.

"For what?" I stared up at him.

"Don't know yet, but when the time comes, you will know," Andre said.

"So bad!" I said as I turned to walk away. "Stop it!" I yelled back without looking back at him.

"Can't help it, it keeps going side to side, side to side," Andre said.

I quickly sped up and closed the door behind me.

I had never felt like this, not with Benjamin, Henry, or others. I was breathing heavily, and my hands felt sweaty.

"MOM!" SHEILA SAID AS she snapped her fingers in front of me.

"Sorry," I said, coming back to reality.

Sheila had come by the house to tell me about her new apartment. I remembered she was saying it was closer to her new job and the college, but after that, I blanked out.

"What were you thinking about?" Sheila asked.

"I can't tell you," I said as I got up and started making dinner.

"You told me about your ex-boyfriend that used you as a cum dumpster, you can tell me anything," Sheila said.

"I hate that description," I said, shaking my head.

"It fits," Sheila shrugged as she started to help me.

I told her about Andre, how he flirted with me, and how I felt about it.

"Back on the horse huh?" Sheila smiled.

"No, it's not like that," I shook my head.

I had planned on being single for a long time, and I intended to stick to it.

"Mom," Sheila said.

"He's too young and, well, he's very young," I said as I continued to make dinner.

"Mom!" Sheila said again.

"And he's not my type, I have never gone outside of my ethnicity, not saying I am racist, but," I said.

"Mom!" Sheila said.

"The age difference alone, but he is so funny, and the way he talks," I said.

"Mom!" Sheila said as she reached over and shook my hand.

"What?" I asked.

"You poured flour into the dish, when it's supposed to be salt, unless you're putting lasagna into that pan and not that one, you're messing it up and last time I checked ketchup isn't pasta sauce," Sheila said as she pointed out everything I had messed up.

"What the hell!" I said as I looked at everything.

"I'll order pizza," Sheila smiled. "You should call your boy toy!"

"He's not my boy toy!" I yelled back at her.

"Uh-huh," Sheila said. "Don't drink your wine, it's olive oil!"

I looked at the glass in my hand, and sure enough, the olive oil bottle was near to me, and the wine bottle was still in its place near the fridge.

"Call him!" Sheila smiled.

After, we had dinner and a few wines. I promised Sheila I would stop by her apartment tomorrow. I was left alone in the house, and for a while, I just stared at the card Andre had given me.

"Just a text," I shrugged. "Simple text."

'Hi,' I sent.

"There's it's done," I said as I felt better.

'About time, was wondering if you were going to give me the cold shoulder,' Andre sent back.

'How did you know it was me,' I replied.

'I don't give out my personal number to everyone,' Andre replied.

We went back and forth for most of the night. Finally, I called him. I had to know what about me he found interesting. Andre floored me by saying he found me alluring and attractive as well as mysterious. Plus, he had to comment on my chest and my ample ass.

"How about I take you out for lunch tomorrow?" Andre asked just before I was about to hang up for the night.

"How about we go to lunch together tomorrow and pay our own ways?" I asked.

"Sounds good," Andre replied.

I hung up, and my thoughts started to linger. Was I jumping from one bad relationship to another? Was I that desperate for a relationship?

'Smile, we are going to have fun,' Andre sent a text.

'Night!' I sent back with a smile.

I tried to get some sleep, but my mind lingered. I had heard everything about dating a black male and wondered if any of it was true.

Before I knew it, I was thinking of sex with Andre. He was much taller than both Henry and Benjamin. He had a much better physique as well. I imagined that large muscular arms around me, squeezing me.

Then it just happened. I reached for my newest toy and started using it, imagining it was Andre on top of me fucking me hard, fast and deep.

I brought myself to two orgasms before turning around and going to sleep.

Chapter Seven: Going for It All

"You know all those rumors are just that, right? Rumors?" Jaquelyn asked as I told her about my upcoming lunch date.

"I am not dumb," I nodded.

"Okay," Jaquelyn said as she looked at me.

"So, what is it really like then?" I asked.

"Same, nothing is different," Jaquelyn nodded. "Nathan is the same as Derek, Andy and all the other men I have been with, all of them have minor differences, but all the same within reason."

I nodded. I was prepared for something if things went further than just a lunch date.

"What are you thinking about?" Jaquelyn asked.

I didn't want to tell her exactly what I was thinking. It had been the same thing I was thinking about last night and this morning.

"Ah," Jaquelyn smiled as she looked at me through our video call. "Sex with a black man," she laughed.

I didn't know what to say.

"Like I said, it's not different, if that's what you are thinking then you are wrong, like I said before Nathan isn't huge or does he last all night, or cum buckets," Jaquelyn smiled. "He is just like all the others."

I was slightly disappointed. I had thought it might be different.

"Don't look so disappointed, your guy might be different," Jaquelyn said.

I didn't want to get my hopes up, but after being with Benjamin and then Henry, I wanted something different, something more exciting.

Maybe that's why I had such an interest in Andre. He was different from both Benjamin and Henry.

"There is that look again," Jaquelyn said. "What are you thinking now?"

"Nothing," I smiled. "I will call you later."

I did have something in mind, but it would have to wait until later. I had to head to work and get things ready for a sale that I worked on.

"So, what's the issue?" Sheila asked as she met me at the house I was trying to sell.

I told her about my lunch date, and Sheila smiled from ear to ear. "I knew you would call him," Sheila smiled.

"It's just lunch," I shrugged as I set most of the furniture and other pictures that I usually placed in a house.

"Then why call me?" Sheila asked. "Could've gone on the date without telling me anything."

"I just wanted to make sure you were okay with it," I said.

"I was the one that told you to call him," Sheila said. "So, of course I am okay with it. What's the real reason?"

She had me, there was more that I wanted to know, and as much as I didn't like asking my daughter about personal things, she did have the most experience.

Unlike Debra and I, Sheila was more promiscuous. She didn't see herself as the settling down and getting married type. Debra married Jimmy straight out of high school, and I married Benjamin in our first year of college. Debra had only been with Jimmy her whole life. Benjamin and Henry were my only experiences.

"Ah," Sheila smiled. "Sex!" she laughed.

"You don't have to be that loud," I shook my head.

"What do you want to know?" Sheila asked. "If it's the whole big black cock thing, that's a myth and only for porn."

"Really?" I asked.

"Definitely, trust me, four black guys only one was above average, and the whole can go for hours thing, yeah, that's a lie too," Sheila shrugged. "They were a bit more assertive and aggressive, but other than that," Sheila shrugged.

"Same thing Jaquelyn said," I said, slightly disappointed again.

"One thing I do like, is the color difference," Sheila nodded. "It's probably what turns most white women on the most, and there is a certain taboo to the whole thing."

"How so?" I asked.

"The looks people give you when you're out with a black man, and the slight whispers and people shaking their heads," Sheila smiled as if she remembered something. "It's quite exciting."

"Even in the city?" I asked.

"Anywhere," Sheila shrugged. "Movies, dinners, restaurants, just walking around, it's a rush. You will see."

I didn't think about that aspect. I had never thought about it, but now that she brought it up, I remembered Henry shaking his head at an interracial couple as we were dancing. Benjamin always thought it was a traitorous act to have a mixed child.

"You think it will go that far?" Sheila asked.

I didn't know for sure. We hadn't even gone out yet, and here I was thinking about the next step. Maybe all Andre wanted was to go out.

"My advice?" Sheila asked.

"Absolutely," I nodded.

"He's younger than you and doesn't know everything you have been through, so take it slowly this time," Sheila said.

"Go slow, coming from you?" I smiled.

"I am just saying, you're looking for something that he might not want," Sheila said.

I nodded. I didn't need another failed relationship. I wanted something more substantial, something real.

"Thanks," I nodded.

"Anytime," Sheila smiled.

"SO, WHERE ARE WE GOING?" I asked as I met Andre in the parking lot outside his building.

"There," Andre pointed to a Caribbean restaurant across the street.

I had seen many people going in and out of it, but I had never gone in. I had to admit I had no interest in the food, let alone the loud music from the restaurant.

"Ah," Andre said. "Don't knock it before you try it."

I nodded. We walked across the street and into the restaurant.

Immediately all eyes fell on the white woman with a tall, dark-skinned man. At first, a bit of fright and fear came over me, but as Sheila said, the excitement slowly came over me as we sat down.

A huge black woman came to the table, put down some menus, and asked what we would be drinking. Andre smiled at me as I looked over the menu, trying to look for a regular soda.

"Cream Soda, is the closest you will get to a sprite," Andre smiled.

"Fine," I smiled back at him.

The woman walked back behind the counter as I looked at the menu. There was nothing that sounded appealing, except for the curry chicken which I had at an Indian restaurant.

When the lady returned, I placed the order, and Andre smiled back at me. "What?" I asked.

"Next time you can pick the place," Andre said as he leaned back in his chair.

"Next time?" I smiled.

"I am hoping there will be a next time," Andre said.

I knew there would be the next time before the lunch was over. Andre was a smooth talker, not like Henry, who mainly talked about himself and listened to me when I spoke.

Andre was different in that he asked questions. He challenged me in a way no other had before. He asked about my job, how things worked, how I got it, and what was the most challenging. By the end of the lunch, he knew more about me than Henry did when we dated.

"What about you?" I asked as we both paid our way.

"How did you like it?" the lady asked as she gave me a box to put the rest of it in.

"Fabulous," I said. "Especially the rice, never had it like that before," I nodded.

I was full to the gills and didn't even eat half of what was on my plate.

"Hope you will come back," the lady said.

We walked outside, and I felt the total weight of what I had eaten. "I mean it," I said.

"It will have to wait for next time," Andre said. "Or unless you call me later?"

There it was again. He was putting everything in my hands. With both Henry and Benjamin, it was 'call me,' or 'text me,' with Andre. He was making sure I was the one that made the decisions.

"I will text you, when I get off, I have a few more errands to run, but after that, I am free," I nodded.

"Then I will wait for your text," Andre smiled as he stood by the door.

I started to walk over to my office. "You're doing it again!" I shouted.

"Definitely," Andre yelled back.

A smile crept over my face knowing Andre was staring at my ass as I walked away.

"How did it go?" Sheila asked as I finished up the last of my errands and was returning home.

"Excellent," I replied.

"So, will there be more?" Sheila asked.

"Most definitely," I nodded. "You were right," I smiled as I pulled up. "There was a lot of stares."

"I told you!" Sheila said. "Exciting, isn't it?"

"Beyond words," I said, remembering the people's looks in the restaurant and crossing the road.

"What about the assertiveness?" Sheila asked.

"He's so confident and the way he talks, makes me want to talk even more," I said, sitting in my car.

"Bet he asked if you would call," Sheila said.

"How did you know?" I asked.

"Happens every time," Sheila said. I could hear her smiling on the other side of the phone. "I told you, it's a lot different to what you're used to, and more."

"Well, I told him I would text him now," I said, looking at the time.

"Well, you better hop to it," Sheila smiled.

I went inside and put the leftovers in the microwave to be heated up, then changed. I ate and then sat on the couch.

'Back home,' I texted.

'Good, how did everything go?' Andre replied.

"Nope," I said, shaking my head.

I was about to take this bull by the horns. I called, and Andre immediately picked up. "Nope, your turn to talk," I said, laying down the law.

"What do you want to know?" Andre asked.

"Everything," I said.

"That's too broad, you're going to have to ask," Andre said.

There it was again. Putting things in my hands. I sat up on the couch and wondered where to start. There was so much I wanted to know. Before, all I did was sit and stare, and Henry told me everything. It came out like someone had opened a damn, and all the water came out.

"How did you start your business?" I asked. It was a safe first question.

That question led to other questions, and before I knew it, we were going back and forth. I would ask something, and then he would. Andre loved that I liked to cook and wanted to know what my favorite thing was to make. I loved that he enjoyed working with his hands and that his uncle had taught him everything from the ground up.

I learned that he had got in trouble with the law at a young age and that his uncle raised him after both his parents passed away while he was young.

Before I knew it, the time had flown by, and I was still on the couch at three in the morning. The sound of my phone dying finally made me realize how long we had been talking.

"Lunch tomorrow?" Andre asked as we both were calling it a night.

"My turn," I nodded.

"Okay," Andre said.

When I went to bed, I fell asleep as soon as my head hit the pillow.

DATING ANDRE WAS NOTHING like I had expected. I told him about my divorce, which he knew nothing about, and my relationship with Henry.

We both decided to take it slow as he had also been cheated on. His ex-girlfriend slept around on him with many others right under his nose.

Andre had never been married and had no kids, which when I told Jaquelyn and the others, they were shocked. There went the other rumor about them getting women pregnant and then leaving them high and dry.

For the next month, we went out to lunch and talked all day and night. I wasn't getting much sleep, and it wasn't a bad thing. I looked forward to curling up in bed every night and listening to him talk. One night, he fell asleep while on the phone with me, and for a while, I just listened to him before turning the phone off. Andre apologized profusely the next day.

"I can't get over it," Alexander said in the office one day.

"What?" I asked.

"That," Alexander pointed at me.

I knew what he was talking about the look on my face. The others had pointed it out as well. There was a permanent smile on my face. I didn't know how not to stop. Andre was always on my mind. When I wasn't on the phone with work or Sheila, I was texting or calling him.

"Well get used to it," I shrugged.

"Aren't you scared?" Kelly asked.

"About what?" I asked.

"There are a lot of women that go into that store," Kelly said.

I shrugged. "And guys," I nodded. "Andre is good at what he does, my car is proof."

I loved the tints and the rims and a new stereo system that Andre had put in. He worked with his cousin and one friend, especially during the weekends, as it always got busy.

"So, you don't think he would cheat?" Kelly asked.

"Watch," I said. I picked up my phone and texted a simple hi. I held my hand and put up the numbers in order 1,2,3, and there it was a text back. "Every time." I said.

I looked at my phone and laughed immediately. It was a large panda gif, and the panda was waving.

"I trust him," I nodded. "More than anyone I have ever dated, he doesn't give me a reason not to, he tells me where he is going at all times, and never asks me where I am."

"Never?" Kelly asked.

"Never," I responded. "He trusts me."

"Must be nice," Kelly nodded. "Ian asks me every time when I am getting off, where I am going, who with, and why?"

"Sounds like your married," Alexander responded.

"Sounds like he doesn't trust you," I added. "I went out with the girls the other night and we drank too much so we had to get a hotel, Andre said just be safe and have a good night."

"A full night out with the girls and he didn't question why you were staying overnight?" Kelly shook her head. "Ian would have a heart attack."

"Because Ian doesn't trust you," Alexander said. "I trust Helen, to do whatever she pleases, and vice versa. That's what a real relationship is about, the trust not to ask where, who, what and when."

"You did that with Benjamin and look what happened," Kelly said.

Alexander nodded at me. "She does have a point there," he said.

I nodded. "Benjamin and I had our life together, and you're right I did trust him not to, and he took it and ran."

I couldn't put my finger on how this was different. I just knew in my heart that Andre, as young and very handsome as he was, wasn't the type to cheat, not that we had done anything but hold hands and go dancing.

I loved that about him. There was no pressure. Henry wanted to get in my pants from the first date. Benjamin was in my pants the moment we started dating, and here I was nearly two months into dating Andre and not one attempt, sure, he grabbed my ass and put his hand in my back pocket when we walked together, but it wasn't an attempt to fuck me.

"I am just saying, I have seen the looks some of those women give him, when he walks by, or drops you off," Kelly said. "He is very good looking."

"And that's why Ian asks you the questions he does," Alexander nodded.

"I can admire someone's looks without thinking sexually about them," Kelly smiled.

"You've thought about it," Alexander pointed and laughed.

"You have not!" I said, shocked that my co-worker was thinking sexual thoughts about my boyfriend.

"Before you guys were dating, yes," Kelly admitted.

"Well, cleanse those thoughts," I shook my head with a smile.

We all laughed about it and then went back to work.

I WAS WALKING WITH Andre through the grocery store. I loved cooking for him because he always ate everything I cooked, taking most of it home with him.

The same looks always made me smile, especially when we held hands, kissed, or showed any signs of affection.

Sheila was right about one thing it was infectious. I could understand why other women went out of their way to date outside of their ethnicity. It was such a rush that I would give looks back or add a simple smile, which always added flame to the fire.

'Where did he go now!' I thought as I walked around looking for Andre.

I told him to get some black pepper, and now I couldn't find him. I was about to text him when I felt a hard slap on my ass.

"Ouch!" I playfully said as I knew it was him.

"The guy over there says you have a nice ass," Andre said as he put a few things in the cart.

I turned to see one of the stockers embarrassingly looking away. "It's okay, he's mine," I said to a lady with a flustered look on her face.

Henry would be jealous if someone told him that his girlfriend had a nice ass. As for Benjamin, he always hated that my ass was so big, loved my tits, but hated my ass.

"I can't believe you did that," I said as we got in the car.

"What, he was staring around the corner of the aisle and I wanted to know what he was looking at," Andre shrugged.

"So, he told you and then you came and slapped my ass?" I asked.

"No, he said what he would do with a woman with an ass like that," Andre smiled as he pulled out of the parking lot and headed towards my house.

"No!" I laughed.

"Yup, he said he would be slapping that and hitting it from the back, so I said I would go and slap it for him," Andre laughed.

"Poor guy," I shook my head.

"His fault," Andre shrugged.

As usual, Andre ate a full meal before leaving that night. I always worried about him until I got a text from him that he had made it home.

His small house was in a bad neighborhood, and as much as Alexander and I told him we could get him a better place at a reasonable price, he didn't want to leave the neighborhood, not until his uncle had passed.

His uncle was very sick, and it wasn't going to be long until Andre would be saying goodbye, but he said he was prepared and that even though it would be hard, he was ready for the day.

"You're wearing that?" Sheila asked as she came by the house to pick up some new things for her apartment.

"Yes, why?" I asked.

"You lean the wrong way, or make any sudden moves, they might pop out," Sheila said, pointing at my chest.

"Andre keeps paying attention to my ass, I am trying to point out that I have large tits, he can pay attention to as well," I said as I pulled up my top.

"I think the whole bar is going to know you have tits, and they might get a full view of them," Sheila said as she shook her head.

I looked in the mirror. "Maybe I am over doing it," I said, looking at the top that I had picked.

My tits were spilling out in every direction. "Not a maybe," Sheila said, shaking her head. "Lean forward," Sheila ordered.

Sure enough, both my tits fell out of the top. "Okay, point made," I said as I went back to my closet.

"The white mesh top that you wore to Debra's birthday party!" Sheila yelled into my room.

"Good idea!" I yelled back.

It was see-through enough to show the goods but without exposing them. I took another look in the mirror and was satisfied. *If this doesn't get his attention, then I don't know what will,'* I thought as I went downstairs.

Jaquelyn and the others were bringing their boyfriends along, and we were all going out of town for the weekend. The first night was a bar way out of town, then we were going to the beach and then taking a flight to Vegas.

Even Sabrina was bringing her fabled perfect gentlemen she had met online.

"Wow, look at you," Sabrina said as we were the first ones at the bar.

Andre and the rest of the guys were meeting up somewhere and then coming together. Somewhat of a male bonding process since most of the women knew each other beforehand.

"Think he will finally notice them?" I asked.

"If he doesn't then you know he's not interested in boobs," Sabrina nodded.

"Holy crap Alison!" Jaquelyn said as she arrived. "Think people on the moon can spot those things."

"Should've seen what I was going to wear before I changed my mind," I laughed.

The night was in full swing before the men finally showed up. By the looks of things, they had already started drinking.

"Who was driving?" Francis asked. Always the one to be the most responsible.

"Me," Andre said. "I promise I didn't drink anything."

"Party pooper," Nathan slurred as he walked over to Jaquelyn.

"Nope, just responsible as always," I said as I pulled Andre next to me.

"Woah!" Andre said, staring down at my cleavage.

"Finally!" I shouted.

"Have you always had those?" Andre asked, literally staring at my boobs.

"Yes! The whole time!" I nodded.

"No!" Andre shook his head.

"He's been drinking!" Sabrina and Jaquelyn said in unison.

"Keys!" Francis yelled.

"You ruined it!" Gary said. Sabrina's internet lover.

The rest of the night was a nice mix of getting to know each other's counterparts and dancing. I loved to dance. Andre was not bad at dancing, but he wasn't a lover of it. We were all sore and ready to head to the hotel by the night's end.

"Stay," I said as I held Andre up next to the door.

He might not love to dance, but he loved to drink. And the other older guys loved watching my poor guy take shot after shot.

"I think the floor is moving again," Andre said.

"No, it's you," I smiled.

I prodded him against the wall outside of our room and quickly opened the door.

Slowly I got him inside and onto the bed.

"Sorry, I ruined your night," Andre said.

"Babe," I said, holding his face. "You made my night, didn't ruin it."

"Seriously?" Andre asked.

"Yup," I smiled. "I couldn't be happier. Now I am going to get our clothes and stuff from the car, if you have to puke try and make it for the bathroom."

"Okay," Andre nodded.

I went downstairs and into the parking lot. "Boyfriend, okay?" Francis asked as she was heading for her car.

"Yeah, yours?" I asked.

"Don't ask," Francis said, shaking her head.

I could tell Francis and her boyfriend was already at ends. The guy was a total flirt. He flirted with Sabrina right in front of all of us. He blamed it on the drinks, but we could tell he was serious.

Gary and Andre had hit off, which I was surprised, I thought Andre and Nathan would be more of a friendship, but Nathan kept calling Andre his son, which just rubbed Andre wrong, but Gary was just like Andre, quiet at times and loud at others.

I got back up to the room and heard the loud snoring. *At least he's not puking everywhere,* I thought.

I had to get him out of those clothes. He was sweating right through them. "Babe!" I said as I tried to get him to wake up. "Well, that's not going to work," I said.

'Not the first time you have to strip a drunk man,' I thought to myself as I rifled through Andre's suitcase and found bedclothes.

I had to undress Benjamin countless times after coming home after going out. Unlike Andre, Benjamin was a much bigger man. While Andre was taller, Benjamin was much broader all around.

I easily maneuvered Andre to get most of his clothes off until it came to his pants and underwear. "Well, then," I said out loud.

I finished changing him and set the A/C to a lower temperature. Then I went out on the balcony.

"Mom?" Sheila said, barely awake.

"Sorry to wake you, but I just wanted to tell you, that you were wrong," I said.

"About what," Sheila said.

"He does have a large one," I said, shaking my head.

"Seriously Mom, you called me at two in the morning to tell me your boyfriend has a big dick?" Sheila said.

"Yes," I replied.

Sheila hung up, and I started laughing.

Chapter Eight: Settling Down

So, I was wrong," Jaquelyn shrugged. "There is always one that out of the bunch."

We all laughed as we sat on the beach. It had been a long drive out here, but it was nice to see the ocean. Francis had picked a wonderful place, it was small and quiet, but the view was beautiful.

As usual, the guys were off doing their own thing while the rest of us women took in the sun and the view.

"Did he pound you into submission?" Cassandra asked. She and Timothy had met us at the resort this morning.

"No," I said, very disappointed, I had moved my ass all over the bed and onto Andre's crotch, trying to get him to take me, but he was too damned polite. Even this morning, I tried to make attempts, but I got an ass grab, and then he was in the shower.

"Maybe he is being polite, you did tell him you wanted to go slow," Sabrina pointed out.

"Not at a snail's pace," I shook my head.

The rest of them laughed. "Gary took the hint," Sabrina smiled.

"I heard," Jaquelyn shook her head. "The walls of that hotel are paper thin!"

"No, you didn't," Sabrina replied in shock.

"Oh yeah," Jaquelyn nodded. "Surprised a man that skinny can make a big woman like you scream that loud."

"Oh, he works wonders with that tongue of his," Sabrina smiled.

"Come on," Cassandra said, shaking her head. "Too much information!"

"Oh, like you didn't tell us all about Timothy and his stamina," Francis shook her head. "Timothy can go for hours, he hardly ever needs a break," Francis said, mocking Cassandra.

"Well, he doesn't," Cassandra smiled. "He's like the energizer bunny, keeps going and going."

"What about Drake?" I asked Francis.

Francis shook her head. "I am sure he thinks about other women, mainly you," she said, looking at Sabrina.

"I told him last night, to stop, I was pretty adamant, and so was Gary," Sabrina said.

Drake had been hitting on Sabrina again this morning. As soon as we got here, he had tried to lay on the charm. It wasn't like Sabrina was better looking than the rest of us. I was sure it was because she was the youngest.

Nathan was a few moments away from kicking his ass. When Jaquelyn had to restrain him, Drake took the hint and returned to their room.

Andre shook his head and didn't want to talk about it. He felt sorry for Francis.

Later Drake apologized and said it wouldn't happen again and that he was overly friendly. But I knew he was just upset that he had been caught and that Sabrina wasn't falling for it.

The day progressed well, and later that night, we all went to a local restaurant. The food was exquisite, and even Jaquelyn and I laughed at the looks some of the locals gave us. Of course, Jaquelyn, who was always one to stoke a fire, told two locals to take a picture because it would last longer.

The older man shouted back that were traitorous bitches, and we should be sorry for what we were doing. Of course, Andre and Nathan wanted to stand up for us, but we had it covered. By the end of the conversation, the older man and his wife were leaving the restaurant while Jaquelyn and I laughed.

After finding him flirting with one of the younger waitresses on the pier outside the restaurant, Francis sent Drake home. Drake wasn't too happy about being shown the door.

"Sorry about Drake," Andre said as just the two of us walked the shoreline.

"What's to be sorry about?" I asked.

"I know you guys wanted this to be a good weekend," Andre said.

"It's an excellent weekend, Drake did nothing to ruin it," I shook my head. "There are good guys and bad guys, good women and bad women," I shrugged.

I told him about my dad and how he raised four children on his own after my mother decided she didn't want to be a mother anymore. One day she went out for groceries and never returned. My father had been the cornerstone of my life.

Andre hardly knew his parents, but he said his uncle raised him the best that he could.

We walked back and forth along the shoreline, kicking our feet in the water and enjoying each other's company.

Finally, at midnight we decided to go back to the room. This time I was going to make sure that Andre knew I wanted something to happen.

Earlier this afternoon, most of us went into the small town and went shopping. I picked out something sure to turn Andre's head.

I had never bought anything so revealing and risqué in my life, and even as I looked in the mirror, I didn't know how he would react. I wasn't like Jaquelyn, Francis or Cassandra; I didn't have the type of body that something like this would look sexy on. I had a big stomach, thick thighs and an enormous ass with huge tits.

Lingerie never was meant for big girls, but I wanted to make sure that Andre knew that I wanted more, and I was hoping this did the trick.

"Well, here we go," I said as I opened the bathroom door that led to the bedroom.

Andre was watching something on television and didn't turn his head right away. I slightly coughed, and Andre turned to look at me.

Immediately he stopped and stared, and his eyes went wide.

"It looks horrible, doesn't it?" I asked. Unsure if it did the trick or not.

The television turned off, and Andre reached forward and grabbed my hand and pulled me to the bed.

"Okay, so it did work," I smiled as Andre's hands were all over me.

I barely had time to react before I was naked on the bed next to him. Andre had magical hands that turned my engine from idle to full

throttle, if that wasn't the end, he started kissing my way down my body.

I didn't want to think about it but or him, but Henry's feeble attempt came shooting into my head, but it went flying back out as Andre's tongue worked itself into me. Andre lifted my vast legs and dived face first between them.

I had never felt anything like what came next. It felt like nothing I had been through. I grabbed the top of Andre's head and pulled it towards me as he continued to use his tongue, face and fingers to get me off.

The moment I thought he would stop was when he would push further.

It felt like I was about to explode internally.

"Yes!" I screamed, digging my nails into the back of his head.

I had watched videos of women that came like this but never thought it would happen to me. My body reacted to Andre's actions. The first one came fast, then another right on its heels. Before I knew it, I was cumming hard, over and over.

I felt terrible for Andre as I squirted on his face and over the bed, but he acted like I had done nothing and was still going.

I had to beg him to stop so I could feel my lower extremities.

"Did I do something wrong?" Andre asked in the most innocent voice.

I kissed him hard, wet face and all. I couldn't care less. He had done something that I never thought was possible for me, at least.

"Okay," I said as I started to lower myself.

Andre's cock was massive, not just long, but very thick. There was no way this thing would fit into my mouth. Even trying as best as I could, its head barely got into my mouth, with both hands wrapped around it.

I had an idea, and I quickly got into position. Leaning slightly forward and placing Andre's legs on either side of my torso, I managed to get his dick at chest level.

"Wow!" Andre said as I wrapped my big tits around his cock.

'Got ya!' I thought as I saw the familiar sight of a man in heaven.

I bounced my big tits up and down his cock, making sure to lick its head as it popped out from between them. I loved looking at Andre as he tried to stop himself from cumming. The more he tried, the harder I bounced my tits.

I watched as his black cock disappeared and reappeared between them and knew he wouldn't last much longer.

Just as I thought, a few more minutes went by, and Andre thrust his hips upwards and came between my tits. It looked like a geyser shooting warm white liquid onto the top of my tits.

We went to bed in each other's arms, and I smiled as he wrapped his arms around me and squeezed my tits. 'Finally!' I thought as I fell asleep.

The Vegas trip was a total bust. The flights were delayed both going there and coming back. And as much as I wanted to get laid, it didn't happen. I ate something that didn't agree with me, and I was laid out in bed for the whole night.

I tried to get Andre to go with the others, but instead, he chose to stay with me and watch re-runs of television shows. Since it was his first time in Vegas, I felt sorry for him, but he said he had fun playing nurse.

THINGS DIDN'T GET BETTER when we returned. Andre's uncle turned for the worse and had to be put into hospice. A few days later, he passed away. Andre was heartbroken, but he kept a strong face and powered through most of it.

I met some of the family, and they were happy to see that Andre had finally met someone that showed an interest in not just him but everything about him.

I helped Andre pack the tiny house. Alexander, Derek and I promised him we would fix it up without changing too much and make sure it went to good people.

Another thing happened that surprised me. I was on the way home from selling another house when I got a call from Benjamin. It was out of the blue and very unexpected.

We talked for hours about the changes in our lives. Benjamin no longer practiced law. Instead, he was an intown truck driver hauling goods for a large warehouse chain in California.

I was shocked when he said he lived in California now. He also had no interest in politics, either running or paying attention to what was going on. Which blew my mind as he was always glued to the television and conservative radio.

Then he broke it down to me that he had remarried.

Benjamin sent me a picture of his new wife. She looked good, much thinner than me, and had long brown hair. They looked good together.

That's when I told him about me, first about Henry, which he had a good laugh about, and joked about me dating a cop. Then I told him about Andre.

At first, there was silence, and I expected the talk about dating outside my ethnicity, but I heard crying instead. Then Benjamin started apologizing for everything he had said and done while we were together and how his new wife had opened his eyes to everything around him.

They had gone backpacking across the country, and he got to see different walks of life and how people lived, and it made him feel small and his ideas insignificant to the grand scheme of everything going on around us.

I had to smile and called him a hippie. He laughed and said he would never have seen things like that, but he was happier now and wanted me to tell the children to reach out to him when they felt like it.

I knew just talking to him, Debra would be interested. As for the rest, it would take time. Especially my guard dog Sheila, she would be the last to contact him.

Andre took some time for himself and closed the shop for a while. He went back to the islands to be with some of his other family, but we stayed in touch, and he promised he would return soon. I understood that he wanted to take his uncle's remains back home.

The holidays came up fast and furious, and we all decided to rent a cabin in the mountains, away from everything. Andre laughed at me when he returned, and I told him we would go skiing and camping.

"Black people don't ski," Andre laughed as we got up to the mountains.

"Sure, they do," Sheila smiled. "I have seen plenty at the Olympics," she laughed.

"We don't claim them," Andre smiled.

"What too scared?" Mason asked.

"Scared of hitting a tree, yes," Andre replied.

"It will be fun," Pamela said. "Just avoid the trees and the cliffs."

"That's it, I am going back home," Andre laughed.

We all laughed and joked for the first night in the large log cabin.

It was nice to see the family having fun. Even laughing as loud as we could. Even the grandchildren liked Andre. The younger ones loved playing elevator with Andre's muscular arms, they would hold onto his arms, and he would lift them off the ground.

I went out onto the balcony and saw Mason holding a warm mug.

"Thoughts?" I asked as I joined him.

He was the oldest of my kids by only a few minutes, but he was always brooding or thinking about something.

"You're happy," he said, looking at me.

"Absolutely," I nodded. "That a bad thing?"

"I came up here expecting to talk you out of this," Mason said, turning to look inside as everyone was having fun. "I thought you were just jumping from one bad relationship to another."

"Sheila thought the same thing, and for a while so did I," I nodded. "But he's good for me, and good to me, I promise."

"I can see that," Mason nodded. "For the first time, even when you were with Ben, I feel helpless," Mason said.

"Helpless?" I shook my head. "You have always looked out for us, all of us, now you have someone to share that responsibility with, he isn't taking it away from you, or trying to replace you. Talk to him and you will see that he would love to share the load with you."

Mason nodded. "I am just happy that you're happy for a change," he smiled.

"Very," I nodded as we hugged. "Now, let's go inside it's freezing out here."

Mason and Andre did have that talk the next day, and for once, I saw Mason smiling next to a man I loved.

Skiing wasn't Andre's forte as he fell many times before Jimmy and the others told him to quit while he was ahead.

We spent Christmas in the cabin sharing gifts and eating dinner. And unlike the last one, when we parted, it felt almost too short.

Andre and I took the flight home while most of the others were taking the long drive back home. I had houses to get back on the market, and Andre wanted to open his shop.

"So, I did good?" Andre asked as we sat on the plane.

"Wait until we get home, and I will show you," I said as I lay my head on his shoulders.

Andre kissed my forehead, and I fell asleep. I loved him more than I loved Benjamin. He had done the impossible. All of my kids and their counterparts loved him and the grandkids; we had to take poor Taylor off him as we left because she didn't want him to go.

I told them all about Benjamin, and as I thought Debra volunteered to be the guinea pig and talk to him, the others were skeptical, but she was always the one to give someone a second or third chance.

"So, we are home," Andre said as we got settled down at my house.

Andre had moved in, and although I thought it would be a terrible mistake moving this fast, it proved to be the best thing possible. Of course, there were slight hiccups here and there, but nothing is ever perfect.

"Bedroom, now!" I said as I ordered him up the stairs.

"Now?" Andre asked. "Don't you want to...."

I gave him a look, and we sped up the stairs.

Clothes came off in a flurry of movement. Since that night at the beach, we hadn't been together, and I couldn't wait any longer to know what it felt like to have his large cock inside me.

It didn't take long, for as soon as we got onto the bed, and I laid out on my back. I felt the large head of Andre's huge cock at the entrance. He rubbed it up and down, teasing me. "Put it in!" I yelled.

Immediately I gasped as the total size stretched me to the limit. I hadn't even got the head of it, and I was already clawing at the sheets.

"Go slow," I said as Andre pushed more of his monster cock into me.

I reached for and started sucking on my nipples as more of his cock pushed into me, filling me, stretching me. I looked down as Andre put my legs onto his shoulders.

Sheila was right. The color contrast was terrific to see. I watched as his black cock entered me and couldn't believe I had only taken less than half of it inside of me. I shook my head and urged him to put more of it in.

Andre slowly pushed deeper into me, and it felt like he was in my stomach.

"There," I said as it started to hurt more than it felt good.

Andre started fucking me, never going further than I wanted him to. He paid attention to me as I began to love the feeling of his large cock pounding into me repeatedly.

Andre stopped suddenly, and then he grabbed my legs and twisted them.

'Of course,' I thought, as I got on all fours. He wanted to see my ass bounce off him.

"Not in my ass!" I warned him.

"Of course not," Andre said as he entered me from behind.

Again, I gasped as his large cock started pounding my insides. Andre grabbed my hips and started pulling me back onto him. Then he slapped my ass while fucking me.

For a man in his forties, he had stamina as he kept going and going.

Then I felt it, the slight twitch. Then it happened again. Andre was about to cum, I waited to feel him filling me with his cum, but he quickly pulled out and came on my ass.

"Why did you do that?" I asked.

"I didn't know if you wanted me to," Andre replied.

"I definitely wanted you to," I nodded with a smile.

"I have never stayed inside," Andre admitted. "Not without protection."

"Honey, the baby factory has been closed for many years," I smiled.

"You can cum inside as many times as you want."

Instantly I saw his cock throb as I said that. I smiled and knew it wouldn't take long for another go-round.

I was right. Andre had many turns to cum inside me that night and every other time. And after a few months, we were doing it everywhere we could, and I took more of it into me each time.

I finally felt his large balls slapping against me the other night as he fucked me from behind, Andre's favorite position. I loved being on top, but both of our favorites was me tit fucking him. I still couldn't get it in my mouth, but he didn't mind.

"AND FOR YOU, FROM ME," Sheila said as she handed me a present.

It was my birthday, and all the women had thrown me a surprise birthday party. No men.

I quickly opened it and saw that it was a shirt. It said, 'Andre's Cum Dumpster!' in bold print on the front.

At first, I shook my head, and then I nodded. "I like it," I nodded. "Can you get it in black and white, green and white isn't our color?" I said.

"Mom, it's a gag gift," Sheila said, holding another present.

"I know, but I really want one," I nodded as I folded it up. "Preferable a black shirt with white writing."

"You can get the writing in liquid, so it looks like it's dripping!" Jaquelyn said.

"Yes!" I nodded.

"You should put that spade emblem on the back, and you can wear it outside," Francis said.

"I am definitely wearing it out," I said.

"Guys, it's a joke," Sheila said, shaking her head.

"I want to get one now," Sabrina said. "But with Gary's name on it!"

"We should all get one," Cassandra nodded.

"Different colors," I nodded.

"Guys, seriously, you can't wear them outside people will stare," Sheila said.

"Next Vegas trip!" Jaquelyn flicked her fingers.

'Yes!" we all said in unison.

Sheila shook her head. "I can't with you guys," she said as she looked at us.

I hugged my daughter. "You love us," I smiled.

"I do, but seriously no wearing these shirts out," Sheila said.

"Watch us," Francis smiled.

Later that night, I wore just the shirt as Andre got out of the bathroom. He took one look at it and jumped onto the bed.

I love being Andre's cum dumpster.

The

End

Also by Alexander Martin

Crossroads
Crossroads: Time Waits For No One

Office Relations
Office Relations: The New Boss
Office Relations: Helpful Boss

Standalone
A Better View
A Different Kind Of Summer
A Dish Served Cold
A New Direction
Snowed In
A New Helen
Bull By The Horns
A New Life

About the Publisher

Alexander Martin is the pen name of my Erotic Stories. I love writing. My Erotic Stories dive into my wild side. Most of the stories that you will find under my pen name involve interracial relationships and the pros and cons of being interracial.

Read more at https://medium.com/@alexander-martin/lists.